"If you need anything, just call," Jim said quietly, standing in the hallway clad only in a pair of low-slung jeans.

Marybeth slipped her gaze upward, past his bronzed, muscled chest to his eyes. "I will."

He caressed her cheek. "Is there a reason a friend can't kiss a friend goodnight?"

"No," she whispered, lifting her face. He slid his arms around her and kissed her passionately. It left them both wanting more.

"This is nuts," he said. "Come back to my room with me."

"Not in your father's house," she said.

"Then we'll sleep outside," Jim suggested.

She sighed. "Not here, not with our parents in the house."

"Marybeth, I'm not trying to win a medal for good behavior," Jim said, yanking her to him in a fierce embrace.

She kissed him back, then eased out of his arms with a soft sound of regret.

He gripped her arms. "Take the thought of me holding you naked in my arms to bed. . . ."

WHAT ARE *LOVESWEPT* ROMANCES?

They are stories of true romance and touching emotion. We believe those two very important ingredients are constants in our highly sensual and very believable stories in the *LOVESWEPT* line. Our goal is to give you, the reader, stories of consistently high quality that may sometimes make you laugh, sometimes make you cry, but are always fresh and creative and contain many delightful surprises within their pages.

Most romance fans read an enormous number of books. Those they truly love, they keep. Others may be traded with friends and soon forgotten. We hope that each *LOVESWEPT* romance will be a treasure—a "keeper." We will always try to publish

LOVE STORIES YOU'LL NEVER FORGET
BY AUTHORS YOU'LL ALWAYS REMEMBER

The Editors

540

Doris Parmett

Unfinished Business

BANTAM BOOKS
NEW YORK · TORONTO · LONDON · SYDNEY · AUCKLAND

UNFINISHED BUSINESS
A Bantam Book / May 1992

If you would be interested in receiving protective vinyl
covers for your Loveswept books, please write to this address
for information:

Loveswept
Bantam Books
P.O. Box 985
Hicksville, NY 11802

ISBN 0-553-44248-1

Published simultaneously in the United States and Canada

PRINTED IN THE UNITED STATES OF AMERICA

OPM   0 9 8 7 6 5 4 3 2 1

For Elizabeth Barrett. A great editor.

Unfinished Business

One

Marybeth Wynston hated calculators. She considered them cold, impersonal harbingers of bad tidings. Find ten thousand dollars or stay in debt, hers told her.

Six months earlier she had tried everything she knew to sell the pottery she had custom-made for a design house that had declared bankruptcy before paying her. Then her landlord had raised the rent on her small shop. Bills had mounted until her only recourse was to close up shop and move back to her mother's home, a casualty of the country's economic recession. She was determined, however, to succeed one day.

It was bad enough she had failed at love. There she was, temporarily washed up at twenty-five. How many women her age could claim two major disasters in five years? First she'd lost James, then her business.

She had met James in Chicago during her senior year in college. A dashing charmer with a sense of humor, he'd swept her off her feet. At the time he sold restaurant supplies. Big, bold, brash, beautiful James, who knew he was going to be a success. He'd set her on fire, and she had gladly given him her virginity, her heart. Madly in love, she'd moved in with him, certain they were destined for each other, until—

"Marybeth."

Her mother's voice jolted her out of her reverie.

Marybeth put on a smile and turned from the stove as her mother walked into the kitchen. "Hi. You look terrific in that yellow jump suit. No older than thirty-five."

Charline Wynston was a tiny package of dynamite, a daintily determined woman with baby-blue eyes, shiny blond hair, and a figure that kept its shape no matter what she ate. She presented an image of sweetness, but given the right circumstances, she could be a barricuda. Mess with her child, mess with her. In her syndicated newspaper column, Charline, aka Henrietta Heartfelt, dished out advice with humor, common sense, and a sharp wit.

"I made chicken soup for lunch," Marybeth said. "Or I can heat up leftover spinach pasta."

"I'll have soup. Not too much, please. Marybeth, there's something I have to say that will surprise you. I'm leaving this afternoon for the Catskills for ten days. With a man. Watch the soup ladle!"

It plopped into the steaming pot of chicken soup.

"Did I hear you right?" Marybeth cried in amazement.

Charlie fished the ladle out of the soup. "Sit down, dear. We'll chat."

Marybeth sank into a chair at the kitchen table. "But why haven't you said anything before?"

"I wanted to see where this was heading first. Or maybe I wanted to hug all of it to myself." She set a bowl of soup in front of her daughter. "I wish you'd fall in love, Marybeth. Dennis isn't the right man for you. He's nice, you're nice, but you're not nice together. You don't set off sparks in each other. You need to find a man who does."

Marybeth bit her bottom lip, staring down at her soup. James had set off sparks. James had set off a conflagration! She'd never told her mother about him.

"Forget me," she said. "Who is this guy you're running off with? Does he wear an earring and ride a motorcycle? Wear black leather pants?"

Charlie laughed with delight. "No, but he does wear sexy mirrored sunglasses. He's State Police Sergeant Gerry Matson, and he's an artist with the Crime Detection Unit."

Charlie sat down at the table with a bowl of soup for herself. "We've dated for over a month. He lives in an apartment here in town, and up in the Catskills he owns forty-four acres of land with a ten-acre lake, a floating dock, a rowboat. That's where we're going today. He said he'll teach me how to fish." Charlie deliberately paused to eat some soup. "Who knows?" she added casually. "We may decide to get married."

"Married!"

"Don't get upset, Marybeth." She smiled at her daughter. "I said *may*. Be happy for me." She dipped her spoon into her soup. "I left Gerry's address and phone number on my desk upstairs. Call only in an emergency."

Marybeth was staring at her. "I can't believe I'm hearing this. How did you meet him?"

Charlie smiled in memory. "He tried to arrest me."

"Arrest you!"

"I was doing seventy in a fifty-five-mile zone. After that I sort of forced him to pay attention to me. I took

one look at that six-foot-two-inch hunk and something clicked. He noticed a six-pack of beer in the
car. He wasn't impressed when I told him I bought it
for company, and ordered me to take a sobriety test."

She chuckled. "'Ma'am,'" he said, 'walk ten paces
forward, then ten backward. Seven to the right,
seven to the left.' That's part of the sobriety test."

Intrigued, Marybeth leaned forward.

"He made me do the walk, then recite the alphabet
backward. So I did it in French. He called me a sassy
little thing, told me I mispronounced the *u*, and to
purse my lips next time. When I zipped past him the
second time, he raised his arm out the window and
pointed to the side of the road, signaling me to stop.
He leaned into my car window—rugged face, sexy
mouth, mirrored shades, and enough potent masculine impatience to get my motor running. Gerry
oozes sex appeal. He asked me whether I was addicted to speeding or just plain crazy."

"I can see why."

"You should try it sometime, darling. When you
meet a man who's so—"

"Go on, Mother."

"By then we were laughing. 'Really, Gerry,' I said.
'People are looking.' He told me not to spoil his fun.
He asked the name of my perfume. When I said
Entrapment, he grunted and said, 'It figures.'"

"Did he ticket you?" Marybeth asked.

"Of course not. He just likes to see me wiggle my
tush when I do the sobriety walk." Marybeth couldn't
help smiling. "He let me off with a stern warning,
then he tracked me for eight miles. Before turning
off, he pulled up alongside my window and tipped his
hat. I winked. He laughed. I haven't felt so good in
years."

"What happened the third time?"

"He merely honked his horn. I already knew to pull over. He read me the riot act, but by then we both knew we were hooked. He ran the tip of his finger, just one superior swipe, down the length of my nose. I never knew there could be so much raw talent in the merest touch. I knew the routine. I did the walk, and I wiggled. After that we went for coffee. If I hadn't been speeding, I never would have met him."

Marybeth was astounded. She burst out laughing. "You're incredible. You, of all people. You usually drive like a turtle!"

"I couldn't chance losing him. That's what I meant about setting off sparks in each other. It's been years for me."

Marybeth thought of James, of how he melted her with a look. He didn't even have to touch her. One special look, a visual heated message, did it for her. Her mother sounded as excited about Gerry as she had felt about James.

"When I return we'll concentrate on you," Charlie said, finishing her soup. "It's high time we put our heads together and come up with a plan. In the past few years you've misplaced your joyous, bubbly personality. When you become a mother, you'll understand why I can't be truly happy unless you are."

"Confine yourself to the lovelorn column, Mom. Don't be Henrietta at home. Are you sure you want a man with a dangerous job?"

"Gerry's retiring soon." Charlie sighed and stared across the room, her chin propped on her hand. "I love his sense of humor. And he makes me feel like a precious jewel he carries in his pocket for safekeeping."

"Does he know how much money you have?"

Charlie looked at her daughter again. "We don't

discuss bank balances. He knows your father abandoned us and then died when you were a year old, that we lived in New York City until I bought this house five years ago. He doesn't know I'm Henrietta Heartfelt, the columnist."

"Why not?"

"I'm no different from other successful women. I want a man to love me for myself, not for the trinkets I bring to the party. I'm telling him this week."

"If he's a cop, don't be so sure he doesn't know everything there is to know about you. Retirement takes money. What about him?"

"He's divorced and has a stepson. He'll be arriving for a visit when we return. Gerry's retirement party is the following week."

Charlie glanced at her watch, then pushed back from the table. "Gerry will be here in a few minutes to pick me up." She smoothed her jump suit over her hips and looked at Marybeth. "I'm nervous. Does that sound foolish?" She gave her daughter a hug. "Wish me luck, and try to understand. And remember, Marybeth. Don't settle."

Marybeth had a vision of herself years before, sharing a bed, a home, a life with James. Long after she had kissed her mother good-bye, long after she had cleaned the kitchen, long after she had finished working for the day, she thought about James. Her mother's advice, "Don't settle," haunted her.

Jim Davis finished reading the quarterly report his secretary had placed on his desk. Despite the country's economic woes, business was good. He slipped the report into his briefcase, then checked to see if there were any minor details he needed to attend to. In a few minutes a reporter for the *Courier* would be arriving to interview him. He'd be happy to talk about the success of his chain of fast-food restaurants, called Quick Stop.

As soon as the interview was over, he was flying to New Jersey, where his stepfather, Gerry Matson, lived. Not only was he eager to see him and help him celebrate his retirement from the police force, he himself needed time off from his fast-paced schedule of the last two months, when he'd held meetings with the managers of his restaurants in ten different states. He firmly believed in personally keeping in touch, in hearing firsthand the problems his employees might have. But he needed a break and this was a good time to take it. He was flying east a day before his dad ended his vacation—a vacation he was taking with a woman named Charlie. His father had sounded so excited when he'd called Jim two weeks earlier to tell him, and Jim was eager to meet this woman.

Jim's natural father had died when he was a baby, and his mother had married Gerry when Jim was three. His mother, however, hadn't been able to take the strain of being a policeman's wife, and had divorced Gerry twelve years later. Jim and Gerry continued to see each other, though, valuing their father-son closeness.

Jim's secretary, Nora Fischer, knocked on his office door and entered. "The reporter from the *Courier* is here."

He nodded. "Okay. I'm done here, Nora, so you can leave. Thanks for coming in on a Sunday."

"No problem," Nora said. "I'll send the reporter in."

He spent the next half hour answering questions, praising his loyal staff, discussing the use of recycled materials in his fast-food restaurant, and how he was expanding the menus to include meals for the increasingly health-conscious population.

The reporter smiled at him and crossed her legs. "That takes care of all of my questions about your business, Mr. Davis. I'm sure our readers will be interested in how you spend your free time too. You're an attractive man as well as a wealthy one, and you no doubt have a very active social life. Is there a special woman in your life?"

There had been, he thought. A picture of a young girl floated through his mind.

He was kissing her belly. She was laughing.

"I'll make you stop laughing in two seconds," he told her.

"Try it," she said. "I dare you."

He lowered his head and kissed her intimately. She gasped. Clutching his shoulders, she urged him on, begging for release. The laughter turned to moans of ecstasy.

"Mr. Davis," the reporter said. "Would you care to discuss your social life?"

"No," he said bluntly, standing to signal the end of the interview. "You know what they say about all business making Jack a dull boy, Miss Patterson. That's me."

Then he remembered to smile.

Dennis Jorden paced Marybeth's den. She had told him nine days earlier about her mother going off with a man. Personally, he envied the man his success. He'd tried and failed with the daughter. At least tonight Marybeth's mind was on other things, eliminating her plan to read Shakespeare aloud. The things he did for her!

"What's wrong with entering the contest?" he asked, returning to his earlier suggestion. He waved the Quick Stop circular in the air. "There's no sin in it. You wouldn't be breaking a holy convenant. You'd simply be trying to win so you could pay your debts."

Clad in a denim skirt and cotton blouse, her hair loose about her shoulders, Marybeth sat on the couch cuddling her cat, Peaches.

"You shouldn't eat in those places, Dennis."

He didn't bother telling her that for dinner that night he had sinfully consumed a double burger with cheese, bacon, mayo, lettuce, tomato, and a large order of fries. Dating Marybeth came with restrictions.

"There's a ten-thousand-dollar top prize," he said, "for the best nutritious recipe for a main dish. It's perfect for you. If anyone knows how to prepare a healthful meal, it's you. Enter one of your pasta dishes. You might win. You said yourself you can't wait until you pay your debts and move out. What have you got to lose?"

"My chances of winning a contest for a fast-food restaurant equal my chance of winning the lottery. Is that ketchup on your shirt? Ketchup's full of sugar."

"I don't care. You're not my mother, or my sister. What you're supposed to be, Marybeth, is my girl-friend. But you keep holding me at arm's length. Some nights you won't even let me hold your hand, much less kiss you."

Frustration forced him to be honest with her. "I like you, Marybeth, and I thought we had a chance. But you're carrying old garbage that I can't fight. I strongly suggest you find the guy and clear up your unfinished business with him."

Thrusting his hands into his pockets, he stared hard at her. "Look, I know that behind your uptight façade you're a terrific woman. A sensual woman. I've seen flashes of it. I'd like to have a deeper relationship with you, but not at the cost of reading Shakespeare aloud and eating pabulum."

Marybeth's mouth dropped open. This was a new Dennis. She winced. No, this was the *real* Dennis, the one she had refused to see for the two months they'd been dating. "Do you eat any healthful foods when you're not with me?"

"Not on purpose. I'll be dead a long time. I'd like to enjoy my life while I'm here. You might as well know I'm allergic to cats too. I've been taking shots. I see nothing romantic about walking in the rain and getting wet, and I can take ballet only in small doses. Personally I prefer football, rock and roll, and real ice cream."

Marybeth sighed. She swung her head back and forth, her long hair swaying with each motion. Her shoulders trembled with laughter. Peaches jumped off her lap and ran for cover.

"You poor man." She looked up at Dennis. "I ought to sleep with you as penance."

A grin tugged at his lips. He held out his hand. "Let's go."

She waved his hand away. "Dear, dear Dennis. You're a wonderful, intelligent, fine man. With your blond good looks, the way you fill out your clothes, you're dynamite. A heartthrob. For someone else. My mother said we were wrong for each other, and she's right. You shouldn't settle for a woman like me. My differences attracted you, but given a taste, you'd return to ordering from the regular menu. The fast-foods menu." Her eyes twinkling merrily, she flashed the Quick Stop flyer.

"Marybeth, you're not entirely sane, are you?"

She chuckled. "Probably not. But at least I can now see that if we got together permanently, we'd be snarling at each other within a month. I love walking in the rain. The opera. Museums. Ballet. Yogurt. And I could never part with Peaches. She was given to me a long time ago by . . ."

"A man?"

She smiled up at him. "He's unimportant. I'm totally over him. He never really was important, except as a first love."

Dennis rocked back on his heels. "First loves are potent. Are you sure about us, though? I could keep on with the shots."

She shook her head. "I really don't think it would work. Can we still be friends?"

He nodded, and she felt a huge sense of relief. She followed him to the door, and just as he put his hand on the knob, the doorbell rang. He opened the door, then moved aside for her. She uttered a low cry when she saw the man standing there.

Jim locked gazes with the tall, shapely woman framed in the doorway. Her chestnut hair was longer, curling impudently around her shoulders, but her cat green eyes were the same, as were the classically oval face and lithe body he had kissed thousands of times. In the five years they had been apart, the raw desire he'd felt for her had mercifully changed from sharp, knifelike pain to a dull ache, a constant companion in his heart. In order to be able to work, to carry on his daily activities, he had forced himself to concentrate on the good times, not the awful memory of their parting, feeding his fantasies of one day seeing her again. But in those fantasies he'd never imagined her as more beautiful than she'd been. He never would have thought that possible.

"Hello, Peaches," he said.

James, Marybeth thought. No other man in the world called her Peaches. As unbelievable as it was, he was standing on her doorstep, tall, trim, and terrific. Her heart somersaulted as questions tumbled through her mind. Barely breathing from the shock, she forced herself to calm her rioting emotions. Five years had added to his rugged he-man demeanor. Wide-shouldered, his hair dark and thick, he riveted her to the spot with the heated expression in his hazel-brown eyes. Beside her, Dennis's polite cough jarred her out of her trance.

"Hello, James."

He smiled, and her stomach plummeted. His gaze flicked briefly to Dennis, whose arm lightly rode her shoulders. His smile faded.

"What . . . what are you doing here?" she asked.

Jim could smell her alluring scent. Did that man next to her kiss the places where she dabbed the perfume, as he had? He pushed his hands into his pockets to keep from grabbing the man by the neck and tossing him off the porch. He wanted to be alone with Marybeth. A public reunion was not what he'd had in mind when he'd driven over there.

"I just flew in from Chicago this evening," he said. "I dropped by my dad's place in case he'd gotten back early, and I saw your mother's picture in his bedroom. I recognized her from the snapshots you carried. I know my dad's dating a woman named Charlie, and that woman, Marybeth, is your mother."

"My mother!" she exclaimed. "And your father?"

"My father, that is, my stepfather, is Gerry Mason."

Marybeth's breath whooshed out of her lungs. "My

mother and your stepfather! Gerry Matson's your stepfather? But you have different last names."

He shrugged. "Gerry wanted to adopt me when he married my mother, but she preferred I keep my natural father's name." Jim frowned as he watched the other man gather her close, as if to absorb her shock. Or to flaunt his right to touch her.

He went on. "To say I was surprised when I saw your mother's picture is putting it mildly. How do you think I feel about my dad dating your mother?"

Misinterpreting the root of his censurous tone, she stiffened. "I can hear how you feel. You'd think after so long you'd stop prejudging people!"

"That's not what I meant, dammit."

"Call me stupid, but I go by what I hear."

"Marybeth!" Dennis said. "Who is this guy?"

"Sorry." She quickly introduced the two men.

Dennis stared at Jim, then at her. "How long have you known him?"

Her chin lifted defiantly. "We met when I was in college. My mistake."

A look of dawning came over Dennis's face. "Is he the guy you said you're over?"

"Yes."

Dennis began to laugh. "Did he have anything to do with your naming your cat Peaches?"

"Of course not!"

"You're damned right I had something to do with it!" Jim said. "I gave her that name. Ask her why. Ask her under what circumstances!"

Marybeth felt her cheeks burn. Those circumstances were as intimate as two people could get. They were making love on the floor before the fireplace in his apartment. He said she tasted like peaches and cream. All over.

"How dare you?" she exclaimed. "That's personal!

Extremely personal! And don't you dare call me Peaches! My name is Marybeth. I didn't know what to expect when you showed up at my door, but I can assure you it wasn't to hear you judge my mother! Your dad isn't here and I refuse to listen to another word from you."

Her face beet red, she stepped back into the house and slammed the door in both their faces.

Dennis sat down on the top step. Jim, furious with himself and yet unable to stop, lunged for the doorbell. She yelled for him to go away. He banged on the door.

"Not so fast, Peaches. Open the damned door or I'll call the cops."

"Do that, James!" she yelled. "Call your daddy!"

Dennis angled his head upward. "Wow! That's quite a show you two are putting on. Very adult. By the way, she means it. If I were you, I'd leave."

"Not until we settle this!"

Dennis wiped the look of amusement from his face. "Then may I be of help?"

"Why? What's your interest? Aren't you supposed to be on her side?"

Dennis nodded. "I would be if I thought I had a chance. Apparently she's been carrying burning embers for you all these years. What do you have that I don't? Unless it's that predatory look women seem to prefer this year. What do I call you? Jim or James?"

"Jim. She"—he jerked his thumb at the house— "called me James. She said it sounded distinguished."

Dennis rubbed his jaw. "You don't say. My middle name is Viceroy. That's more distinguished, but she never called me that."

Jim sat down beside him, shaking his head. "If the mother is anything like the daughter, my dad's in serious trouble. All hell is going to break loose."

"From what I can see, it already has. I must admit Marybeth's a lot more vivacious around you. More vibrant. You blinded her to my true personality. I won't make that mistake again. Incidentally, what do you do when you're not inciting a riot?"

Jim told him. Dennis laughed again. "You own Quick Stop? That's rich! Just tonight I urged her to enter your contest."

"Why?" Jim asked, curious.

"Ask her."

"Don't play games with me. I'm not in the mood."

Dennis shrugged. "If her mother and your dad are dating, you'll find out anyway. Marybeth is down on her luck. She's plucky and extremely independent, but right now she's also vulnerable. If you've come here to hurt her, I won't let you."

Jim gave him a hard stare. "How much of an item are you two?" he asked.

"Are you asking if we're lovers?"

"Yes, dammit."

"Are you still in love with her?"

"That's my affair!"

His choice of words brought a smile to Dennis's face. He handed Jim his business card. "I'm always looking for new clients. I'm a damn good forensic accountant. If anyone cooks your books, I'll find the culprit. I'll charge you handsomely too. It's only right. I've had one major disappointment tonight, thanks to you. You stole my girl. Now, if you want the answer to your question, you'll have to give me something in return."

Suddenly Jim laughed, partly with relief at hearing Dennis's admission, and partly at himself as Dennis must see him.

"I'll be damned," he said. "You're defending Marybeth and trying to blackmail me at the same time."

"I'm sad to report we parted pure. Not for my lack of trying, mind you. I can accept your money with a clear conscience. You and my former girlfriend can settle your unfinished business."

Jim stood and lifted his hand to ring the bell once more. "That's settled, then. Now if you'll excuse me, there's a little unfinished business I need to tend to."

Dennis understood perfectly. He had just seen Marybeth angrier and more electrifying alive than she'd ever been for him. One day he would find a woman who felt that strongly for him. He remembered the intense look on Jim's face as he waited to learn whether or not he'd slept with Marybeth. For a man who professed not to care, his tenseness branded him a liar.

Dennis grinned widely. "Sure you don't want me to stay? I'll be happy to referee."

Jim frowned. "Don't push your luck."

Two

Marybeth sat huddled on the living room couch. She must live under an unlucky star, she thought. How could James be back in her life, especially now? Five years, and the first thing he does is insult her mother! As though they themselves had never meant anything to each other, never shared hopes and dreams. She didn't need him messing up her life, or her mother's. The chances of their parents meeting were astronomical. What awful thing had she done to deserve this?

"Nothing," she muttered.

The doorbell rang. She assumed it was Dennis, but she wasn't in the mood to explain. "Not now, Dennis," she shouted toward the door.

The bell rang again.

And again.

She supposed she owed him an explanation. She had acted like a mad woman. What must he think of her? Probably good riddance to bad rubbish.

She had stood and was walking toward the door, when a man yelled, "Peaches, open the damn door!"

Her blood ran cold. For a moment she panicked. Resolutely forcing back the rush of turbulent emotions, she swore this time she wouldn't let him rattle her. Several of her neighbors were members of Neighborhood Watch, and she quickly swung open the door to let him in before one of them heard him and alerted the police.

"Can't you leave me alone?" she asked, slamming the door shut and stalking down the hall. "You've had your quota of insults for the night."

Jim expelled a harried breath and followed her into the kitchen. "I told you I wasn't trying to insult your mother. You took it the wrong way. Weren't you shocked too?"

"Yes, but I didn't condemn your father."

In his wildest dreams Jim couldn't have picked a worse scenario. In his best dreams he'd envisioned her coming back to him, sobbing that she couldn't live without him. In his arrogance he never imagined she'd slam the door in his face.

He'd made a mess of things.

"Peaches!" he cried, momentarily diverted by the cat who padded up to him. She arched her back to rub his leg, then began to lick his hand furiously. "You've grown, Peaches."

Peaches purred.

Marybeth tossed her hair over her shoulder. Her namesake was a traitor. She was obviously enamored of the man who used to scratch her tummy and feed her.

"Peaches," she said crossly, "leave him alone. James, why are you here?"

He straightened from petting the cat. "Relax, for goodness' sake. Don't you think we should discuss our problem?"

She crossed her arms. "I don't consider my mother

a problem. On the other hand, I don't know your father."

"If you trust your mother's judgment, you'll know he's a very nice man."

"Love can distort a woman's good sense."

He threw up his hands. Surrounded by potted geraniums and seeing the herbs that lined the windowsill, Jim thought sourly he might as well be back in their old kitchen. An asparagus fern sprouted abundantly over a hanging metal basket. Small wicker baskets hung on a coat rack. Marybeth put her stamp of ownership on everything. Including him.

He hooked a foot around a chair leg and sat. "I remember the first time I saw you. You were showing kids in the park how to form clay bowls. I was looking for a home for the kitten. You realized I was watching you."

She sniffed indignantly. "Watching? You were staring. Blatantly ogling me."

He smiled. "Shamelessly enjoying myself." He'd gotten a good look at her shapely legs in shorts as she moved around the table of children, offering an encouraging smile to each, reworking the clay if the child hit a snag.

"You marched over to me on your impossibly long legs after about fifteen minutes. Your hair flew and your T-shirt jiggled. You snatched the kitten from me, slapped a ball of clay into my hands, and said I had observed the female form long enough. It was time to try making a figure. You acquired me."

"You pushed yourself on me."

"I was playing for high stakes."

"But you helped the children," Marybeth said, her voice softening for the first time.

"You adopted the kitten. When the college wouldn't

allow you to keep it in the dorm, I took her home with me. I knew you were attached to her and I wanted to get to know you better. After a few months you moved in too. You knew all along I really wanted you."

"Do you still swim?" she asked, wildly casting about for any subject but one that raised fiery images.

"Yes." He leaned back in his chair, lifting the front legs from the floor. Muscles rippled beneath his shirt. "Do you still walk in the rain?"

She nodded.

"I still jog."

Her gaze skittered away. "I gave it up."

"I moved to Lake Shore Drive."

An exclusive address, she thought. She had moved home. "How . . . how is it furnished?" Her voice trailed off. It was insanity to discuss furniture.

His gaze moved from her lips to her eyes. "Mostly white. Stone sculptures on pedestals. The decorator claims the eye moves from space to space. I gave her free reign. Frankly, I didn't much care. It's functional, expensive, and my guests seem to like it."

Including your women guests? she wondered. His place sounded cold, impersonal, not like the man she had known.

"Let's discuss your mother," he said.

She drew herself up tall. "Let's discuss your father."

An almost imperceptible smile flickered across his face. "Peace, Marybeth. I'd like us to be friends."

She gave an unladylike snort. "For my mother's sake, I agree to be civil."

"Don't you think we should discuss our unique problem?"

Hands on hips, she glared at him. "I love the way

you categorize situations. You did that with me, too, when I didn't want to get married at the age of twenty. Marriage and children were for my future. And what did you do when I said I needed time to try my wings? You clipped them!"

Her hands on the table, she leaned toward him. He sensed a desperation in her, as if she couldn't stop the hurt she'd bottled up for five years from spilling out. "Shall I tell you your exact words? 'Go ahead, Marybeth!' you said. 'Throw it all away. Go sow your damn wild oats. Sow a bushel of them. It's all a game to you. A college girl's fling. You like the sex, but you don't love me enough to marry me.'"

"And," he added, his voice soft with hurt, "I said love has everything to do with it. The rest is garbage."

Tears misted her eyes. She pulled back a chair and sat. "So you remember too?"

He reached over to grasp her hand. His eyes were watchful, assessing. "I was your first. A man never forgets that. You trusted me. You were so responsive, so wonderful, I couldn't let you out of my arms.

"That whole first weekend we remained cooped up in my apartment, deliriously happy. We kept the world at bay. Do you remember how often we made love? I couldn't get enough, and neither could you."

She swallowed hard. How could she forget the way they'd been with each other? How their needs kept them coming back for more. She snatched her hand from his. His reaction was instantaneous, and she studied the hard line of his jaw, the dark look in his eye.

"You conveniently gloss over the fact that you threw me out," she snapped. "You tossed me out of your bed. Out of your apartment and out of your life! You couldn't accept my need for independence."

"I was in love with you. I was afraid to lose you."

"So you gave me an ultimatum. You know, my mother married right out of college. I arrived nine months later. I told you my father blamed my mother for having me. That's why he left us."

Jim took her hand again, and when she didn't protest, he soothingly whisked his thumb over the back. "We were using birth control. If we'd had a baby, I would have loved it. My parents were divorced too. I thought what we had was precious."

Although Marybeth had said her mother never complained about being a single parent, Jim had realized later—too late—that part of her reason for refusing to marry him stemmed from her fear of repeating her mother's mistake. Instead of understanding her needs and her fears, he had estranged himself from the one women he loved above all others, the one he wanted to spend the rest of his life with, the one he wanted to hold in his arms each night and wake up with each morning.

He saw the strength and delicacy in her face, the tears swimming in her eyes and clinging to her long eyelashes. He felt rotten. He wished he could wave a magic wand and erase the argument that had incited their parting. He couldn't take back that last ugly scene in his apartment, though, that last ugly fight.

Marybeth grabbed a paper napkin and wiped her eyes, then mindlessly began to shred the napkin. Although they spoke about their painful past, James's very presence was sending a message deep within her. She felt she was symbolically shredding the memory of their parting and paving the way for them to be friends.

"It was over a long time ago," she said at last. "I needed to get it out of my system."

Their gazes locked hypnotically, each wondering who had taken the other's place.

"What did you do after graduation?" Jim asked.

She drew a deep breath, releasing it slowly. "Everything. I traveled in Europe and this country, visiting potters, museums, that sort of thing. I opened a store in a town just an hour's drive from here to showcase pottery, mine and a few other artists'. It was a struggle, but I loved it. Unfortunately with the sluggish economy, it went belly-up."

"I'm sorry," he said, and she heard the sincerity in his voice. "Tell me about it."

At first she was reluctant to, but with his prompting she realized it was safer to discuss business than a failed love affair. She told him about the problems with the now-bankrupt design house, adding, "I had had three accounts fold in as many months, thanks to the recession. I collected some money, but not enough. So when I got the large order from the design house, I was delighted. Euphoric. The buyer insisted every piece be custom made. He wanted to advertise them as one of a kind.

"Then things fell apart. The landlord raised my rent. I was losing twenty-five percent of what I fired due to the clay cracking or imperfections in the glazing, and I could produce only six or seven custom-made items a day. Then the design house declared bankruptcy. Everything that could go wrong did. My rate of fixed and mounting expenses far exceeded the trickle of orders coming in. It was a case of getting in deeper or bailing out. I bailed out."

"When did you move here?"

"About six months ago. My main concern is to sell the large quantity of stock. My poor mother's house has odd-shaped boxes all over the place. Each item has to be packaged separately. Lamp bases, vases, and bowls take up room. With no cellar and a full garage, she's being very patient."

"Do you think you'll have a problem selling the stock?"

"Probably. I had advised the buyer to vary the merchandise, to select old country pottery, cobalt blue spongeware and saltware, Chinese style Raku, or Indian southwestern designs. He insisted instead on the brown and neutral tones popular in the sixties and seventies."

"Why? Surely he wanted to make money."

"He thought he was right. He was totally convinced the neutrals and browns were about to make a comeback and he'd make a killing. It was his decision. After all, I was merely the supplier. If I didn't fill his order, another potter would. He wanted to take delivery all at one time, so I didn't even receive a partial payment. I have," she said wryly, "temporarily joined the ranks of the new poor."

Despite her casual tone, tears filled her eyes. She quickly rose and turned away, standing with her back to him. He stood, too, and stepped in front of her. His hands gripped her arms.

"I wish it could have been otherwise, Peaches."

"The book isn't closed yet," she assured him, blinking away the tears. "I'll turn things around. Thank goodness I learned from my mother the importance of being able to stand on my own two feet. I've mailed out portfolios of my work and placed an ad in the local papers. Tomorrow I'm taking more stock to Diana McGill's store."

"Your college friend lives here?" he asked, surprised to hear her name.

"Yes. Diana owns a small gallery and jewelry boutique in Flemington. She accepts things on consignment, rotating the ones that don't sell after a month or so. She drapes gold necklaces on my vases for window displays. Besides her, I try selling at shows."

Jim raked a hand through his hair, fighting the urge to take out his checkbook and hand her a blank check. He wanted to protect her. It hurt him to see her dreams dashed. Her brave smile didn't quite reach her eyes. From the first moment he'd seen her he'd felt fiercely protective of her, and that was still true now.

"Does your mother know about us?" he asked.

She eased away. "No. If you recall, she was in England then, researching a book. I had intended to tell her in person. Then we . . ." Her shrug spoke volumes. "Does your father know?"

Jim shook his head. "Right after we broke up I took a job with a company that led to my first Quick Stop restaurant. Between searching for a site for the restaurant and getting it up and running, I didn't see Gerry for six months. He knows I had been in love and that it didn't work out. Frankly, I wasn't in the mood to carry on a long distance phone discussion about anything other than business."

"It's a good idea if we tell them we met years ago when I was a student. If they knew . . ."

He finished her sentence. "If they knew we couldn't keep our hands off each other, knew we couldn't wait to lock the door and race to our bedroom, it could complicate things for them. And we don't want that, do we?"

She looked away. "No." She focused on him once more, raising her chin and looking him squarely in the eye. "It all turned out for the best for you. You've done well. A successful business, an apartment in a ritzy section of Chicago. I imagine your private life is exactly how you want it."

"Not quite." He flashed her a rueful smile. Mary-beth felt its powerful pull drawing her to its velvet web. Once she could have listened to his deep voice and basked in the glow of his smile forever. She slowly turned away.

Accepting—for now—her unspoken rejection, Jim walked to the screen door. He focused his attention on the backyard that held a barbecue grill, white-and-blue striped lawn furniture, and a hammock attached to a pair of elm trees. "How did your mom meet my dad?"

"Your dad wanted to arrest her."

He swung around. "Whatever for?"

His awestruck expression released Marybeth's laughter. "James, you should see yourself. I was joking. Did you actually think I'm the daughter of a master criminal? My mom's still Henrietta Heartfelt, busy as ever. She still dishes out coast-to-coast advice, and travels to give lectures. Your dad stopped her for speeding."

He looked skeptical. "And invited her on a date? She makes up her mind fast, doesn't she?"

The fragile peace splintered. "It says the same for your dad, so please drop the innuendoes. Besides, it's not her usual reaction. I've never known her to go off the deep end in love. I didn't know they were dating until the day she left. She dropped the bomb-shell right before she took off. At first I admit I was shocked, but then I thought it was romantic."

"Five years ago romance always came first with you. What happened?"

Cursing his ability to read her so well, she met his gaze steadily. "Nothing happened beyond my grow-ing up. Now I'm in a wonderful relationship with Dennis. He's really a terrific man."

Jim's eyes went flat. His nostrils flared. "How is he in bed?"

She gasped. "Don't be crude."

"Answer the question." Jim knew he was being obnoxious, yet he couldn't help himself. It was one thing to think of her with a man he hadn't met; quite another to think of Dennis's hands on her, his lips on hers. He needed to hear it from her.

"Is he as good as me?" he asked. "Better than me? Does he worship your body the way I did? Does he make you purr the way I did?"

"Better," she sputtered, choking out the words. "Infinitely better. In all ways."

He laughed sharply. "That takes care of the sex. How does he kiss?"

"Stop it. You never used to speak this way."

"Answer the question. How does your lover kiss?"

"Marvelously. I melt."

"Like butter? Oh, excuse me. In your case, margarine."

His barb stung. He was the most heartless man she'd ever had the bad fortune to meet. "You're disgusting!"

"And you're a lousy liar." He strode over to her. "Dennis and I had an enlightening discussion."

She stared up at him, seeing clearly the struggle on his hard features. His mouth hovered a fraction from hers. She backed away, despising herself for wanting to pull him closer, to feel the heat of his body, his lips.

"James, you're here to talk about our parents."

"They can take care of themselves. Are you sorry about the past? How we loved each other?"

She didn't hesitate. "When I think of the past, I think of a carefree college student with a bright future. A girl who fell wildly in love with a man she thought of not only as her lover, but as her best friend. A girl who unstintingly and freely gave her love. Perhaps others don't view virginity as a precious gift to give a man, but I did. I could never have gone to bed with you otherwise."

She looked away from him. "I'm all grown-up now, though, with no girlish illusions. I couldn't understand then why you were so intractable. I thought you loved me, really loved me, and knew I was young, needed time. You taught me a valuable lesson."

"What was it?" he asked, feeling an unmanly lump in his throat.

She spoke from a reservoir of hurt, her eyes sad. "Guard your heart. If you don't, it gets trampled. Now, thanks to some fluke of fate, our parents have met. For their sakes, we should be able to be in each other's presence and act like adults."

Regret etched his eyes. How many times, he wondered, had they sat chatting at the table, making plans to go bowling, or to see a movie, or go for a walk? He'd enjoyed whatever they did together. He'd loved her to distraction.

He gazed at her with aching tenderness, searching her beautiful features. He looked into her eyes, and admitted he had to take credit for the cynicism and wariness he saw there.

He nodded, the merest tip of his head. "You're right. The past is past. We'll get through these next few days, then I'll be out of your life."

"Good. If our parents marry, there's no reason for us to meet except at their wedding, and then I'm sure we can behave. I'm glad we arrived at a sensible decision."

"So am I."

They were both lying through their teeth.

"Would you like a cup of coffee?" she asked, proving she could act like an adult with him.

"Please," he answered, casting about for a way to stay longer.

Three

Jim asked for a fourth cup of coffee. Marybeth warned him he'd be up all night.

He flashed her a wide grin. "No problem."

Although she wanted to be serious, she couldn't in the face of his deliberate avoidance of the facts. She reacted with a low laugh. "You know how you get when you've drunk too much coffee. You'll float to the bathroom."

As she bent to refill his cup, her legs brushed his and her scent wafted upward to surround him. Her artist's hands were sure and strong, with long, tapered fingers. He used to watch them delicately mold clay into beautiful forms, her concentration so intent that she would work until her muscles ached and he had to tell her to stop.

"It's easier to be friends than enemies," he said. "For our parents' sakes, of course."

"Of course," she agreed. "Nevertheless, after this cup you're leaving. I've got a busy day tomorrow."

So did he, he mused. He recognized the familiar throbbing she could always elicit in him. His gaze focused on her lips, he put his hand under her chin and lifted her face to his. He restrained himself from reacting to the sudden surge of passion coursing through his body. Old habits die hard, and it was all he could do to keep from lifting her in his arms and carrying her upstairs to bed.

He looked at her with unabashed desire. The creamy softness of her skin had always fascinated him. "Say my name, Peaches."

Captured by his intense gaze, the yearning she heard in his voice, she whispered his name. Then she recalled herself and sat back. "This is pointless. You have to go."

"Spend the day with me tomorrow. We can take a picnic lunch, go to the beach. Talk."

She shook her head. "I don't think that's wise. I already told you I'm delivering a few pieces of pottery to Diana's."

"I'll drive you. I'd like to see her again."

"No."

"Aren't you in the least bit curious about me, about what I've done these past five years? I thought we were friends."

"I already know what you've done. And speaking of friends, I owe Dennis an apology. He's my friend too."

Jim dropped his hands. "I'm a better friend," he said, his eyes darkening. He brushed the tip of finger over her lips. "And I'll prove it."

By the time Jim had driven to his hotel, parked the car, and taken the elevator up to his suite, he had arrived at several decisions.

One: He loved her. He'd never stopped. Two: He wanted her back. Three: He had to prove she reciprocated the first and find out how to get the second. He had the utmost confidence he would. He knew she still loved him. *She* just didn't know it yet. By the greatest stroke of good luck, fate had brought them back together. He didn't expect her to make it easy for him, though. Therefore, he would court her. Their parents might not make that an easy task.

Wired from the caffeine, he remained awake for hours, thinking. He came up with several ideas, and finally settled on one. It wasn't perfect, but it would do.

Despite not falling asleep until nearly two, he was up by six. He figured Marybeth was awake too. She had always been an early riser. He dialed her number.

"Good morning, Peaches," he said when she answered. "I've been thinking about our parents, and I need to see you. I'll pick you up in half an hour. We'll talk over breakfast and you'll have plenty of time to deliver your pottery to Diana." Smiling to himself, he hung up before she could protest.

In her bedroom, Marybeth stared at her phone while her cat rubbed against her arm. "Peaches, he hasn't changed one iota. James, the impatient one."

Minutes later she was washing her face and brushing her teeth. Automatically applying lipstick and combing her hair, she muttered aloud that she had better things to do with her day than be at his beck and call. Had he offered any other excuse than one that included her mother, she wouldn't go. Back in her bedroom, she slipped on a pair of blue jeans, topped it with a baggy shirt, then pulled on socks and sneakers. That was as good as it got at six A.M., she told her reflection. How could James think of eating breakfast at such an ungodly hour? Had he changed that much in five years?

She opened the door for him fifteen minutes later. He strode in with power emanating from each sure step. He looked dazzlingly handsome in a white cotton sweater and beautifully tailored slacks.

"Good morning," he said. "You look adorable."

"I look like a mouse," she blurted out, wishing now she'd taken more care with her appearance.

He chuckled. "The day I think of you as a mouse, I'm in serious trouble."

"Why," she asked, "did you call?"

"I told you. There are matters to discuss before our folks return. It's not as if we have all the time in the world."

He took her arm and, holding her close, ushered her outside to his rented Jaguar. She slid in the buttery tan leather bucket seat and attached her seat belt. The cloudless bright-blue sky promised a glorious summer's day.

"Nice day," he commented as he pulled away from the curb. "Too nice to be cooped up in a house."

It didn't take Marybeth long to realize he intended to wait until they were at breakfast to tell her why he had called. On the way to the restaurant he talked about the summer's first predicted heat wave, and how lucky a person would be to go to the beach.

"How's my Peaches?" he asked after a while.

"I'm not your Peaches."

"I meant the cat." He brushed his knuckles over her cheek and smiled. "You're gorgeous. I'm proud to be seen with you. We're going to my hotel, by the way."

She frowned in disapproval. "Let me out. I am not going to your hotel room."

"The restaurant, Peaches. I'm expecting a call there."

Mortified that she had jumped to conclusions, she

clammed up for the rest of the drive. When they reached the hotel, he helped her out of the car, then they walked across the marble floor of the lobby to the dining room.

"The usual?" he asked her once they were seated.

"No juice for me. It's still too early."

He placed their orders—orange juice for him, tea and toast for both—then sat back. "Last night," he began, "and again this morning I started thinking about what it would mean if our parents marry."

He paused when the waitress brought his juice. He drank some of it, then topped the glass off with water. Watching him, Marybeth smiled in reminiscence. Neither of them drank orange juice full strength.

"Go on," she prompted when he finished it.

"Suppose they have a baby?"

Her eyes widened in shock. "You brought me all the way over here to discuss a baby! What's gotten into you? My mother is forty-five years old and has an active career. I have no idea what your father intends to do when he retires, but I can almost guarantee you my mother isn't thinking about pink booties!"

"I merely mentioned what might happen," James said calmly. "I for one have adjusted to the idea of us being related. Don't you want me for a brother, once or twice or whatever removed?"

"No." A beautiful blonde seated at a nearby table was openly admiring James. He had no trouble getting his pick of women, she thought sourly. "If they marry, you can be the ring bearer."

"You can be the flower girl. Can't you see the two of us walking down the aisle, giving our parents away?"

"You're nuts. Eat your breakfast and take me home."

He buttered a piece of toast. "I have a favor to ask of you, Peaches. I'd like your advice."

"My advice? I don't think our parents need advice."

"Not for them." He stopped eating and reached for her hand. "For me. It's a business matter."

She leaned back in the chair, giving him a penetrating stare. "James, you're successful. I'm in arrears. Doesn't that say something?"

His tug on her hand urged her forward again. He didn't want her to get her back up, but he needed to make his point. "Don't denigrate yourself. Consumer confidence started slipping from the excesses of the eighties. You aren't responsible for the recession. We used to thrash out ideas. Last night you trusted me when you told me what happened to your business. All I'm asking for is equal time. You're a talented, intelligent woman. I value your opinion."

She bit her lower lip. Had she let her image of herself sink so low? She forced a smile, showing him a bright face, changing her demeanor for his benefit.

Silently applauding her, Jim struggled not to get up and drag her out of the chair and into his arms. He smiled into her eyes, proud of the way she quelled her wavering doubts, replacing them with courage.

"Thank you," he said quietly. "Expanding at this time is risky at best. I have to keep abreast of changing habits in food selection. Suppose I added pasta to my menu? Do you think it would bring in additional customers?"

She thought for a minute. "Yes, I think it would. As a matter of fact . . ."

They both became engrossed in a discussion of his idea. He explained the intricacies of assembly-line preparation of meals for millions. Every item was costed out, even down to the percentage of waste in peeling potatoes.

"By leaving the skin on them," she said, "you'll increase nutrition. Pasta should be even more profitable. There's no waste in the cooking."

"You're right." He sent her an engaging smile. "Say, why not make some money on the side? Sell me your pasta recipes."

She sat up straight, her eyes glittering, her voice stiff and defensive. "That's the real reason you asked me to breakfast, isn't it?"

He said nothing for a moment as he considered the gamble he was about to take. "If it were?"

"I appreciate it, but I don't need your help, James."

"Peaches, do you think I'd offer to buy your recipes if I didn't know they're good?"

"You must have a marvelous memory."

It was an incontrovertible truth that for him, she was not only intelligent, she was the most delectable creature on earth. It was also true that he needed to earn back her trust. "I do have a marvelous memory," he said. "For everything. Don't you?"

Marybeth colored as memories flooded back to her. She felt his gaze on her, and she wondered whether he could see her heart hammering in her chest. She slid her hands below the table to wipe them on her thighs, then drained her glass of water.

"James, why did you ask me to have breakfast if it wasn't to offer your help?"

He signaled the waitress. "I like to see your pretty face, but the real reason is that I want you to know I'd love you to be a member of my family."

With that ambiguous statement, he escorted her from the dining room. She half expected him to press her to spend the day with him. Instead, he drove her home, walked her to the door, and thanked her again for her sound advice. He said he didn't want to go to the beach alone, so he'd visit his dad's police precinct to chat with his father's buddies, then stop at a store to buy him a retirement present.

She watched him walk back to his car, her body warming several degrees with the pleasure of feasting her gaze on him. Sleek and handsome, he carried himself with a casual aura of power, of male sexuality. She heaved a long sigh and thought of the blonde who had openly admired him at breakfast.

He opened the driver's door, then looked back at her over the top of the car. "Have a good day, Peaches. My dad's note said they'd be back around eight tonight. I'll see you at six."

She glanced up and down the street to make certain no neighbors were out and watching, then shouted, "James, wait a minute! We have no reason to see each other tonight."

He strode purposefully back up the path. He pulled her into his arms and gave her a scorching kiss that made her knees weak.

He released her. "There," he said, a glint in his eye. "Now we have a reason. See you later."

Now we have a reason to do what? Marybeth wondered as she let herself into the house. Setting aside his request to buy her recipes, the bottom line was that James might want her, but he didn't need her. She'd seen the heated intensity in his eyes. How could she not? Lovemaking had never been their problem. If sex alone defined a relationship, theirs had been in a constant state of bliss. But she needed more than that.

Seated across from him at breakfast did feel good, she admitted. Familiar, like old times, when they batted ideas back and forth in lively discussions. They didn't necessarily take the other's advice. That wasn't the point. The spirited exchange sparked new avenues of thought. But again, she needed more than that.

No, she didn't want an affair that could break her heart. James would be returning to Chicago in a matter of days. Her goal was the same as the past week, the past month. Concentrate on her business and pay her debts.

She climbed the stairs to her cramped bedroom. Anyone who saw it would ask when the movers were coming. Stacks of boxes, containing much of her inventory, lined the floors. All the other rooms, except her mother's bedroom and the bathroom, also held cartons. Due to the odd sizes and shapes of the various pieces of pottery, she couldn't make neat stacks of the boxes.

She carried two boxes to the car, then returned to lug a larger carton downstairs. She put it into the car, rolled her shoulders to relieve the tautness, and locked the front door.

In one respect James was right. On a hot summer's day the beach would be fun. She tamped down a vision of scores of women ogling him in a bathing suit.

Fifteen minutes later she parked in the lot behind Diana McGill's store. She unloaded the cartons, carrying them in two loads through the rear door to the cheerful store. She waved to Diana, who was waiting on a customer buying a pair of marcasite and onyx earrings.

"Why didn't you wait for me to help with the boxes?" Diana asked after the lady departed.

"No problem. How's business?"

Diana shrugged. A big-boned woman with a heart of gold, she rarely minced words. "Fair." She dug into one of Marybeth's boxes and held up a vase. "Mmmm, this one I'll buy for me."

Marybeth snatched it from her and placed it on the counter to be priced. "Don't start that. I'm grateful you show my work." She lifted a bowl from a box. "Di, would you go to a fast-food place if the menu included pasta?"

Diana looked at her in amused wonder. "Who wants to know?"

"I do. James came to see me."

Diana nearly dropped the vase she was carrying to a display shelf. "You're kidding! What brought him back out of the blue?"

Marybeth told her about their parents, adding that James owned the Quick Stop chain.

"Your parents are dating! I can't believe it! Henrietta Heartfelt has lost her heart after keeping it on ice for so many years. But this is great! For you, too, I mean. It'll throw you and Jim together. Honey, if he still loves you, he's your meal ticket out of your financial mess."

"See!" Marybeth whirled from the display shelf. "The first thing out of your mouth is me getting a free ride."

"It is not! You're supersensitive. Super independent. Marybeth, you're not the only one whose dad split."

Marybeth frowned. "What's that supposed to mean? I've never used him as a crutch."

"What about your mom, though? Lots of people use subconscious crutches. How do you think Ziggy Freud got famous?"

"Don't spout your psychology at me. Besides, James is leaving. Our romance ended a long time ago. Why start an affair?"

Diana dusted a curio shelf. "Hey, don't convince

me. I'm not the one in a dither. I'm not the one who fell madly in love. I'm not the one who dated Dennis to ensure she wouldn't fall in love with another man. You are. Convince yourself. Make love with Jim. Prove me wrong."

Driving away a few minutes later, Marybeth discounted Diana's ludicrous suggestion. She had more important things to worry about. Like finding another gallery or gift shop to take the two boxes of merchandise Diana hadn't been able to sell for over a month. It seemed that for every two steps forward she took one step backward.

By early afternoon Marybeth had sold five items through the newspaper ad. It lifted her spirits. Jim phoned, and rather than be irritated at him for his high-handed treatment of her that morning, she told him about her sales. She didn't mention the returns.

After she took care of some paperwork, she decided to take a break from her financial worries. There wasn't anything more soothing than working a block of clay, so she donned a cobbler's apron and went out to the garage, where she had set up her kiln and potter's wheel. Peaches jumped up on a long narrow wooden counter above the wheel. Curling into a ball, she granted permission to her mistress to begin.

Marybeth switched on the radio and a lamp, then took a block of clay, wedging it to remove the impurities. She spent an hour working the clay, sending messages from her brain to her fingers. Testing, forming, reforming, she slapped, rolled, smoothed, and tenderly caressed.

And thought of James. Of skimming her hands over a sleek male form. Of muscles hewn from rock. Of tender caresses.

• • •

His arms laden, Jim watched her from the doorway that connected the garage to the kitchen, admiring her strong, sure hands forming the clay. She bent over her task with single-minded concentration, feeding her talent to the creation.

A soft breeze filtered in the window near where she sat, teasing the strands of hair spattered with droplets of clay. There were more smudges on her cheeks and forehead. Thinking of how he used to help clean her up after a session at the wheel—and what that often led to—he pushed away from the doorjamb.

A shadow fell over Marybeth, blocking the light but bringing with it aromatic air. Swiveling in her seat, she looked up, then started in surprise. Jim's head poked atop an armful of long-stemmed roses of apricot, deep red, alabaster white, and petal pink.

"Don't let me stop you," he said. "I like watching you work."

She rinsed then dried her hands. She hadn't conjured him up. For all the good it did to try to dismiss him from her thoughts, he was there. A presence. Diana would say the gods were conspiring against her.

"Why are you here?" she asked.

"Isn't it obvious?" Jim barely restrained his grin. Before she banked it, he'd seen the flash of irritation in her eyes. Her face, flushed and smeared from work, was fixed in a scowl. She looked adorable.

"I'm here to help you celebrate your sales," he said. "There's champagne in the car."

With the back of her hand, Marybeth stroked beads of sweat from her forehead, then pulled off her apron. Roses were her favorite flowers, champagne her favorite wine. Champagne and roses. Seduction . . .

Working on her manners, she said, "They're gorgeous. I don't want to seem ungrateful, but you overdid it on the celebration. Diana returned two cartons. What am I supposed to do with the flowers?"

"Put them in water and enjoy them." His keen gaze scanned her body. "How much weight have you lost?"

She tilted her head back to look at him. "Thin is fashionable. Haven't you heard? You can never be too rich or too thin. One out of two isn't bad."

"Skinny is out if you've lost weight from worry. You could use a good thick steak."

"Bossy," she muttered. She covered the clay with a damp cloth. Nearly intoxicated by the aroma of the roses, she itched to keep them, knowing that by tomorrow or the following day the buds would unfurl to display their full glory.

"I can't keep the roses," she said with regret. "My mother's due home tonight. She'll ask who sent them."

"You're right. I guess I'll have to throw them out."

"No!" she cried, dismayed at the thought of the lovely flowers in the garbage.

"Have you a better suggestion?"

"Take them to your hotel suite."

He sighed. "All right." He placed the flowers in her arms. "Until I leave, will you put them in water, please?"

She suppressed the urge to say no. She'd give herself a half hour to enjoy the fragrant roses, then send him on his way. In the kitchen she laid the roses on the counter, ran some water in the sink, then found a tall wide-mouthed vase that she had made.

"Have you thought more about selling me your

recipes?" he asked as she started cutting the stems of the roses.

She shook her head. "No. I'm sure you pay good money to chefs and nutritionists. Between them you can get all the recipes you want."

She infuriated him with her logic. She disarmed him with the truth, using it as a shield to hold him at bay. He did pay high salaries to competent chefs and nutritionists. With each negative reply, she thwarted his attempt to get them back together. Swearing at her would be easy. Ranting at her would be a relief.

Instead, he raked a hand through his hair and did what came naturally. He put his arms around her waist and nuzzled her nape, tasting the soft spot at the base of her ear. Her hands slipped beneath the water, fingers flexing. He felt her tension race through her to him. Good. If he had to, he'd drag the passion out of her. That brought a smile to his lips. It gave him hope.

"We can't do this," she said. Her shiver belied her words. He tightened his arms around her waist, melding himself to her.

"I don't pay them good money to make vases." He nipped at her ear. "Sell me your inventory for my restaurants."

She wiggled backward to push him away, but elicited a pleasurable groan from him instead. "I don't want to get involved with you."

"We're already involved. We're practically family."

"We're not practically anything," she said, stuffing roses willy-nilly into the vase. "For all we know, our parents are having an awful time."

"If that were true, they'd have returned by now. My guess is that they've been making love often. Enjoying the discovery of new love. I hope so for my dad's sake. He deserves happiness. Why are you so stubborn? Where is it getting you?"

At his persistence, she dug in deeper. "It's getting me my self-respect, for one thing. For another, I don't need handouts. Especially from ex-lovers. Here." She turned and they were face-to-face, a vase separating them. But needs long denied, needs dreamed of during lonely nights, were pulling them together.

She couldn't afford to start with him again, then be torn asunder when he left. Her reality was finding buyers for her pottery, getting a job to help pay off her debts. "Take this to the living room. Watch it, it's heavy."

He snatched the vase from her hands. He was angry, she realized. Anger she could live with. His brand of gentleness, on the other hand, deceived even as it took, robbing her of thought. He had given her a tiny taste of yesterday. He could be the most gentle man on earth.

She trailed after him with the other vase, which she placed on an end table. He sat down on the sofa and stretched his arms along the back. "Peaches, why do you misinterpret my intentions?"

She rolled her eyes. "Cut to the chase, James. This is me, remember? Do you want to sleep with me?"

A vein throbbed in his temple. "No." Technically, he told himself, his answer was correct. He had something more athletic in mind than sleep. He leaned forward. "Why? Are you asking me to make love to you?"

She blinked. He sent her a charming smile. Pure mischief glinted in his eyes.

"Aren't these flowers for a seduction scene?" she asked.

"They're to celebrate your sales. I thought we were friends."

"Is that what you usually do for a friend?" she asked skeptically. "Kiss her neck, press your body on hers, and buy her dozens of roses?"

"You're remembering our first time, aren't you?"

She blushed. "Don't twist my meaning."

"I'm remembering too. There's nothing wrong with good memories. I spread rose petals on the bed. I wanted it to be special, romantic. Then I scattered rose petals on strategic parts of your body. You remember what I did then," he said, and from the heightened blush on her cheeks, he knew she did. "Same colors as these apricot roses, weren't they? As I recall, you became very demanding within a week."

"I never made demands!" she protested, drawn in spite of herself into the recounting of that first memorable, wonderful, earth-moving experience.

"Yes, you did. Not that I complained. I'll refresh your memory. I bought you roses. We drank champagne. I kissed your fingers. You loved it when I sucked them. I knew. You made catchy little sounds in your throat. Later you said it was erotic. I kissed the corners of your mouth. I did that for me, because I loved it when you turned your mouth hard on mine, thrusting your tongue inside. We heated up fast."

How could he say those things and sit there so calmly? she wondered. He spoke of the heat then. What of the heat now? She was boiling, and just from simple conversation.

"That doesn't prove I was demanding," she managed to say.

Jim shifted in discomfort, crossing his legs. The scenario he'd painted had spiked his temperature. "No, I'm making a point. When I kissed one breast, you demanded equal attention for the other. I preferred to prolong foreplay, but you would get all hot and wet from my touching you and beg me to come inside you. And like a considerate lover, I did. More times than I can count. Isn't that right?"

His lazy smile packed a wallop.

Rising, he walked over to her. His hand slid feather-light up her arm to her shoulder, then curved around her neck, drawing her to him. "Not that you were unfair. You did your share of causing major excitement."

She made a strangled noise. "You're impossible."

"I'm sorry you feel that way." He kissed her on the corner of her mouth. Stepping back, he patted her shoulder. He didn't know how much more he could take. He was driving himself crazy. Caught between annoyance and admiration, he had to find a way to help her clear her debts, free her mind from worry so he could reclaim her.

On the one hand, he was terrified he'd lose; on the other hand, he knew he had to press every advantage at his disposal, including painting mental pictures.

And then there was their parents. They had no idea he knew Marybeth, let alone wanted to marry her. How that figured on the complicated family tree he had no idea. But he didn't care. All he cared about was Marybeth.

Four

Two minutes later Jim was restlessly pacing the room. Marybeth had retreated to the kitchen, manufacturing a sudden desire for tea. He halted in front of a window and gazed outside as he pondered what to do. He was a man who met problems head-on, tackled them zestfully. He enjoyed the art of the deal, of taking nothing and making it into something. He employed people throughout the country. He gave many thousands of dollars to charities. He believed if one was fortunate, sharing with others increased the fortune tenfold. But he wouldn't be able to budge Marybeth until she was good and ready. He felt as if he were climbing a slippery ladder, unsure of his footing, afraid to let go of the rungs.

It was ironic, he mused. Once he had dreamed of the day when money wouldn't be a problem, when he could do as he pleased. Now he'd reached that goal, but he knew he'd remain poor in his heart until he could reclaim his Marybeth.

In the kitchen Marybeth came to a decision. Diana was right. She needed to prove she harbored no lingering feelings for James. She wouldn't need to make love with him, as her friend had suggested. A kiss would do. She had nothing to fear and everything to prove. With her decision made, she returned to the living room. He was standing on the far side of it, his back to her as he stared out the window.

"James—" She didn't get any further.

"You should try selling your inventory to restaurant decorators," he said, not turning around. "They might be able to use a few pieces. A lot of places feature decor from various periods. You've seen the ones with musty old books. There's a restaurant I go to in Chicago that has seven rooms, each decorated in the style of a different decade, from the twenties to the eighties. I can give the decorator a call."

"It's a good idea. Why don't you just give me the telephone number, though, and I'll look into it." She walked up behind him. "Turn around, James."

He did. She was so close, desire flared through him. Her hands slid up his shirt. Until that moment he'd never thought she'd voluntarily reach for him again, let alone boldly assess him. She stunned him with her next sentence.

"I want you to kiss me."

He tipped his head down, his eyes searing hers. "What did you say?"

"I said I want you to kiss me." She traced the outline of his lips with one finger. "Then afterward I want you to go home."

"What's behind this?" Bewildered, edgy, he clamped one hand on her wrist. With his other hand he grasped her hair. It was heavy, dark, lush. His gaze touched her mouth, then dropped to her breasts.

She wet her lips. "I thought you were so in control of your emotions. That is what you were trying to prove before, wasn't it?"

"Funny. I thought it was the other way around, but I've never denied you, have I?" he said in a low, vibrating voice. His disbelief was evident, even while he gazed at her with naked desire. The creamy softness of her skin had always fascinated him. He could sip it forever and not drink his fill.

She stepped confidently into his arms. He lightly kissed her cheeks, her eyelids, then grazed her lips.

"Is that the sort of kiss you had in mind?" he asked, lifting his head.

She blinked. "Uh . . . yes."

"Not me."

His nerves frazzled, he pulled her hard against his chest, crushing her. He seized her mouth in a bruising kiss. There was nothing gentle in how he handled her. His mouth demanded. He consumed her. She pushed him away to take a quick, tortured breath, but then he was back at her lips, denying her a brief respite.

She had wanted to sample a taste, to show him once and for all it was over. He gave her a barrel full of reasons to know it wasn't. She'd never meant to invite this soaring turmoil.

The pressure of lips deepened, as if he feared she might come to her senses even as he lost his. He lost, too, the will to slow down, to savor. The present mocked the past. The woman in his arms was softer, more vulnerable, more desirable, than the girl he had known.

Marybeth shuddered, yielded, opened. He tasted good. There was no other word for it. She threw herself into the kiss, tantalizing him with her gift of giving. His skillful hands molded her to his hard body. His tongue parried with hers, mating with hers. She smelled his cologne, felt the slight roughness of his beard, the hard urgency of his kiss. She felt him.

She had asked for this with her sanctimonious request. He mocked hypocrisy. In the five years they had been apart, she had never tested her ability to withstand his magnetic charm. She ran a hand up his back at the same time he pulled her closer. An electric current shot up her spine. She didn't have the desire, the courage, the will, to break the kiss.

He wedged his knee between her legs, parting them, parting her thighs, while he mesmerized her mouth. He spread his large hand across her chest, seeking, finding the breasts he'd shaped so long ago. He teased the nipple that hardened beneath his touch.

He took her on a frantic journey of rediscovery. She closed her eyes tightly, her arms curving around his shoulders to draw him closer, to feel his sculpted back muscles, to feel that male part of him pressing into her, hard, ready. She drifted down memory lane. She wasn't debt ridden. Hard times weren't on her horizon. She was twenty and in love. Desire, stormy and primal, sped in a swift torrent of sensations.

Breathing hard, he released her mouth. "Where can we go?" he asked hoarsely.

His question brought her sharply back to reality. "No! I didn't mean to start this." She tried to twist away from him. Gasping for breath, she reared back. "It's insane. We can't pick up where we left off as though nothing happened."

He froze. Fighting the sensual haze, he clenched his teeth. "You never used to be a tease."

"You never used to force yourself on me."

"I didn't," he said bluntly. "You came to me."

She drew in a deep breath. She owed him nothing.

She owed herself everything. "I'm sorry for starting it. I'm sorry for leading you on. I don't respect women who tease."

He slammed his fist into his palm, then let out a long breath. He raised a hand to silence her as she opened her mouth to speak.

"Keep quiet, dammit. Stop saying you're sorry. I'm an adult. You didn't force yourself on me. I'm a head taller than you. I outweigh you. You could never force me to do anything. You asked. I knew what I was doing. I wanted to kiss you. For what it's worth, I still want to kiss you. It doesn't matter who asked first. It never did with us. When one of us needed, the other gave. Has it been so long, you've forgotten that too?"

She studied his hard, implacable features. There was fury in his eyes. Fury at her. He thought she'd forgotten. He couldn't be more wrong. She remembered everything. The giving. The taking. The sharing. The loving.

When she didn't answer, he shook his head in defeat. "Just do me a favor, Peaches. I'd appreciate it if you poured me a drink. I could use it. While you do that, I'll dump the water from the vases and put the flowers in my car so your mother won't ask questions."

The plan was simple, she thought. Keep busy. Use your hands for something other than making love.

A lousy substitute.

They'd come a long way, she thought as she wrapped the wet green stems in paper towels. But to where?

Charlie and Gerry had left Gerry's cabin early. A band of hard-driving rain had slammed into the mountains, bringing with it a mess of weather. When Gerry called the weather station he was told that the squall, predicted to hit from their area in the Catskills northward to Canada, was expected to last all night and into the next morning. South of the line, the weather forecaster said, it would be calm, dry, and warm. They packed and headed south, leaving the love nest tight and secure.

"I'm glad you like the house," Gerry said, patting her thigh.

"The best part was being with you. Now we go home and face our kids."

"They're not kids, sweetheart. They're grown-ups."

"Still, I hope they like each other."

"Honey, I'll settle for civil."

Charlie knew what he meant. Children of divorced parents more often than not felt cheated. They were angry their parents hadn't worked it out. They viewed divorce as a form of rejection, of robbing them of their rightful heritage. It didn't matter the age. Often older children had greater trouble adjusting.

"If my guess is correct," Gerry said, "they'll sniff around each other, sizing the other one up. They'll be eager to discuss us. They can't very well do that in our presence. How about a barbecue? I'll bring the steaks. Jim can grill them. Marybeth can be his assistant."

"Marybeth lives on pasta, broiled fish, skinless chicken, and raw or steamed veggies."

He made a face. "What kind of a cookout is that?"

She giggled. "For her, silly, not us."

He relaxed. "Good. I need my strength." He winked and threw an arm around her shoulders for a quick squeeze.

"I worry about Marybeth," she said, remembering

her conversation with her daughter ten days earlier. "I really think she needs a man in her life.

"I'm certain she fell in love her last year in college. When I returned from England, where I'd been researching my book, I found her stressed out and very unhappy. I chalked it up to the pressure of finals, of graduation, of leaving friends she had known for years. It thrilled me to send her on a graduation trip. When she returned in much the same sad state, I suspected there had been an unfortunate love affair. I used to think if I could have gotten my hands on him, I would have personally peeled his skin off for hurting Marybeth."

"Didn't you ask her about it?"

"I know now I should have tried to get her to talk about it. She's a lot like I am. When I was so terribly hurt, I clammed up too. I needed to work it out by myself. Anyway, when she got back, she helped me move into my new house. That kept us busy. Then she started her pottery business and left. As a mother, I'm eager to see her on the right path."

"I know how you feel," Gerry said. "I love Jim like my own flesh and blood. As a kid he'd find stray kittens and go around the neighborhood placing them in good homes. Afterward he'd make house calls to check on the kittens. He's still doing it too. His secretary, Nora, told me that's how she got her cat. But now he spends most of his time running around the country attending to his business. I've mentioned I'd like to see him settle down."

"What did he say?"

"He gave me one of his dark looks, then said he's not interested. Period. He was in love once and he claims once is enough."

"Marybeth thinks she needs a man whose body is a temple to good health, a man who prefers opera to rock concerts, museums to football games. A man who loves to walk in the rain and who rarely gets sick. Germs would be afraid to land on his body, you understand. The man she's dating now, Dennis, is a forensic accountant. They read Shakespeare aloud. They're on *The Tempest*."

"At the risk of being insulting, Charlie, how did Marybeth come out of you? She sounds boring as hell."

"She wasn't always like this. If I could grant one wish, it would be to ensure her happiness. The kind that fairy tales are made of. I'd find her a Prince Charming who would love, honor, cherish, and protect her. A man who will put the spark, the fire, back in her eyes."

Gerry clasped her hand. "The way you've put them in mine. You're still my girl? In the city and the country, right?"

She gazed at him. She loved his open smile, his mature good looks, and the tender memories she carried in her heart for him, "You're the best thing that's happened to me in my whole life, Gerry. You and Marybeth."

"So where are we in this relationship, Charlie? You already know I love you. Why don't we plan our future? There's a stack of travel brochures in the backseat."

"Gerry, I think it's wise to take this slowly. We've both suffered from bad experiences. We know we care for each other, we know we're compatible. After all, we just spent ten days in romantic isolation without one major argument. And the sex was wonderful."

He grinned. The sex was more than wonderful. Their first night, she had shyly confessed that her body didn't resemble the sexy women's bodies on television commercials.

"You're wrong," he had said as he slowly undressed her. "Let me show you how wrong you are." He had lifted her in his arms, laid her gently on the bed, and proceeded to kiss away her anxiety.

"Go on, sweetheart," he said. "You're stating my case."

She smiled at him, but her tone was serious. "Gerry, this is too important for me to make a mistake. My husband had a roving eye. I wasn't enough for him. He also ran up exorbitant bills on our credit cards, and bought a flashy new car we couldn't begin to pay for. I learned to be independent the hard way."

He nodded. She had surprised him when she'd told him she wrote a nationally syndicated advice-to-the-lovelorn column. He was proud of her, yet he'd experienced a pang of disappointment and concern. He was looking forward to retirement, to a carefree and footloose life style, where he could pick up and go on a moment's notice.

"I'd be a jerk," he said, "if I didn't understand. So we'll go slowly—for a while." He gave her a stern look. "But soon, woman, you're going to be mine!"

She smiled lovingly at him, not at all perturbed by his tone. "I just love it when you get bossy," she murmured.

"You two know each other!" Charlie exclaimed.

A few minutes earlier she and Gerry had walked into her kitchen and found Marybeth seated at the table with his stepson. She couldn't be more surprised when the two confessed that they had met in Chicago when Marybeth was going to college there.

Grinning broadly, Gerry hugged Jim, then shook Marybeth's hand.

"I can't believe it," he said, looking at them both. "What a nice surprise! How about that, Charlie? They know each other!"

Charlie nodded absently as she sized up Jim. Tall. Handsome. Totally at ease. Confident. Of course he wasn't as good-looking as Gerry, but then, who was? Her Gerry occupied a class of one. Jim came close though, she had to admit. He shook hands with a firm grip, had twinkling dark eyes and a nice open smile. And she knew from Gerry that he was a kind and considerate man. He was also standing unusually close to her daughter.

Charlie nudged Gerry. "Isn't this nice?"

"Sure is, honey. You say you two met years ago?" he asked Marybeth.

She slid a look at Jim.

"Yes," he said smoothly. "She hasn't changed. When I saw Charlie's picture in your apartment, Dad, and recognized her as Henrietta Heartfelt, I remembered that I'd met her daughter years ago. So I looked up Charlie's address in your address book and took a chance. I recognized Marybeth immediately."

Marybeth smiled. "That's right. Jim gave me Peaches."

"He did? How well did you two know each other?" Charlie asked.

"We met in a park," Jim said. "I was looking for someone to adopt a kitten. She was teaching a group of kids how to form clay bowls."

"Pinch potting. Making bowls. Part of a class project," Marybeth added. "More kids showed up than we expected. We were short-handed."

"I hung around to watch. She enlisted my aid

when some of the kids had difficulty keeping the handles attached to the clay. In return for my helping her, she adopted the kitten."

Marybeth glanced at him and smiled serenely. Inside she was a roiling mass.

"Small world," Gerry said. "But I'm amazed you still remember each other. Did you meet afterward?"

Marybeth stiffened. Gerry sounded like a cop interrogating a witness. Jim, on the other hand, grinned at her. She could almost see the wheels turning in his head.

"Naturally I had to check to see how the kitten was doing."

"That's right," Marybeth said quickly. "He visited the kitten." On cue Peaches padded into the room. She sidled right up to Jim and purred.

Charlie and Gerry exchanged quizzical looks.

Jim rocked back on his heels. "As you said, Pop, it's a small world."

"I'll say." Gerry eyed his stepson closely. Marybeth held her breath. "The kitten has a good memory, doesn't she?"

"Maybe she's related to an elephant," Jim quipped.

"No, she recognizes a person who loves animals," Marybeth said. "Did you two have a good time?" Of course they did, she thought. Her mother was positively blooming.

"We had a wonderful time," Charlie said. "You'd love the place, Marybeth."

"Say," Gerry said, "rather than tell you about it, Marybeth, why don't we show it to you? Charlie and I were planning a family barbecue. As long as you two know each other, there's no reason we can't drive up there next weekend. It's only ninety minutes away and there's plenty of room. How about it,

Jim? You can teach Marybeth to fish, unless she already knows how."

Jim turned to Marybeth and gave her an earnest look. "Would you like that?" he asked quietly.

"Of course she would," Charlie piped up, letting everyone assume Marybeth meant to say yes.

"Then it's settled." Gerry clasped Charlie's hand. "Honey, show me where to take your bags. We'll be right back."

"Now what?" Marybeth asked the second they were alone. "We can't go. No sooner do they return than they can't wait to go back. With us! What do we do?"

He shrugged. "Do you want to hurt their feelings? I don't. I haven't seen my dad this excited in ages. Did you see how they look at each other? We might as well not be in the room."

"I saw. It doesn't change anything. Forget the weekend. I'm sure they don't need or really want us. Your dad either made the offer on the spur of the moment without thinking, or he said it to be polite."

"You don't know that."

"I do. It's small talk. We'd be in the way. Or do you think they'd sleep together in the same bed with us there?"

"How do I know? I'm not their chaperone. Besides, it's a bit late for them to start acting hypocritical. They've spent ten days there. They're old enough to give themselves permission."

She shook her head. "I refuse to go. I can't."

"Then be honest as to the reason." He cupped her chin in his hand, forcing her to look at him. "It's because of us, isn't it?"

"No, it's not," she said, but her cheeks pinkened.

"Peaches, you're a lousy liar." His voice became husky, seductive. "You know I want to make love to you. You could feel what you did to me before. Why pretend it isn't happening again?"

Their volatile reaction to each other was *exactly* why she didn't trust herself to go. She didn't need to jump into bed with him, and that was what had been on her mind for the past hour, ever since they'd kissed.

She shook her head. "I'll find some excuse before the weekend. I suggest you do the same."

"You don't trust yourself with me, do you? What happened to the mature adult who stopped me from making love to you before?"

"I'm smart enough to know not to play with fire!" she said forcefully, then glanced around to make sure their parents hadn't sneaked up on them. She moistened her lips, feeling a noose about to settle around her neck.

Inevitability.

"I want out of this," she said. "Do something."

"What?"

"I don't know!"

Charlie and Gerry breezed back into the brightly lit kitchen.

"It's all set," Gerry said. "We planned everything. All you two have to do is show up. Jim, you're anxious to see the old place again, aren't you?"

Jim felt Marybeth's gaze on him. Not even for her would he hurt his father, who waited eagerly for his reply. He squeezed his dad's shoulder. "Sure, Pop. It'll be like old times."

"Better." Gerry smiled at Charlie. "Infinitely better."

She slipped her hand in his. "Marybeth," she said, "you'll love it there. I promise. You can take long walks. We picked watercress from the brook that feeds the lake. There are so many pretty flowers:

thistles, wild roses, daisies, sunflowers. You're free next weekend, aren't you, dear? It will do you good."

How could she say no to her mother, the tour director? Marybeth nodded.

"Wonderful," Charlie said. "Jim, we'll need two cars for all the things your dad wants to take."

Jim looked at Marybeth with a combination of tenderness and compelling hope. She knew he was in a bind. What she didn't know was that he would have maneuvered for things to happen this way anyhow.

"I'll be happy to drive Marybeth," he said. "I'm counting on it to lift my spirits."

Out of sight of Charlie and Gerry, he winked at her.

Marybeth threw up her hands.

Five

Jim left the bottle of champagne at Marybeth's, took the flowers to his hotel, then drove to his father's apartment. By the time he arrived, Gerry was home. His bachelor pad had two bedrooms, a living room with dining area, a small kitchen, and one bathroom. The men fixed themselves drinks in the kitchen, then crossed into the living room.

Gerry sat in a club chair opposite the television. "You helped me out of a spot back there."

"How?" Jim sat on the couch.

"As long as you know Charlie's girl, you might as well know I asked her to the country for selfish reasons."

Intrigued, Jim leaned forward. "How's that?"

"My interest is in Charlie's happiness. The fact is, I want to marry her but she's dragging her feet."

Jim gulped down some of his drink. "Marriage is a big step, Pop."

Gerry nodded. "And you know mothers. Charlie can't be truly happy unless Marybeth is. I'd appreciate it if you show Charlie how well we get along. As a matter of fact, once we're there, don't hang around on account of us. Invite the girl to an auction or a movie. Show her a good time. For my sake. Mind you, I have nothing against her. I barely know her. What do you think of her?"

Jim's brows raised. In view of the circumstances, he found the conversation unusual. "She's nice."

"Then you'll do it?"

Jim eased back, stretching his legs out and crossing them at the ankles. "Let me get this straight. Are you asking me to date Marybeth?"

Gerry shook his head. "Not exactly. I know you hate being pushed, and I don't blame you. This is different. You're leaving and I'm staying. Charlie's got this thing about family unity. She believes if older people marry and their kids oppose the marriage, trouble follows. So do this for me. Be Marybeth's friend, as friendly to her as you were before."

Jim swallowed wrong and coughed harshly, bringing tears to his eyes. "Dad, you're asking a lot."

Gerry slammed his hand down hard on his thigh. "Jim, this isn't a joke! I already said it's vital for Charlie to see us as one happy family."

One happy family. Jim would like nothing better, but his hopes to reclaim Marybeth were a long way from being realized. When he'd first heard the invitation, he jumped at the chance. But if his dad counted on the weekend to further his romance with Charlie, that would involve Marybeth's active participation. And she didn't want to go. He assumed Charlie would tell Marybeth her feelings on the subject of marriage. Trying to relieve Marybeth of possible stress and added responsibility, he spoke with caution.

"Pop, cancel the weekend. You go with Charlie. Putting four adults under one roof isn't the way to see whether or not we get along. You can accomplish the same thing with a barbecue."

Distressed, Gerry jumped up and paced the small room. "Quit being sensible for once, all right? One time, do it for me. Charlie's no dope. An hour or two of company manners isn't the same as a weekend. When will I get another chance? All of Charlie's evening are tied up this week with speaking engagements. I promised to go with her, but I want time with you too. I'm busy during the day. We all are. Besides, you agreed. If you suddenly call it off, Charlie is going to wonder why. We'll take the boat and fish, get off by ourselves for a few hours."

"Charlie means a lot to you, doesn't she?"

"More than I thought possible," Gerry said seriously. "Charlie says Marybeth's had a rough time. She's ten thousand dollars in debt. That's why she's back home. Also, Charlie thinks a man did a number on her in her senior year in college." He laughed. "Charlie's a real tiger. She said if she could get her hands on the man who hurt her baby, she'd personally peel off parts of his anatomy."

Jim winced. He offered his dad the same advice he had given him years earlier. "You just met the woman. Don't make decisions on the basis of sex. Have fun. Play it out."

"No, with Charlie it's more. She's the woman for me. Fate brought us together. I'd like it if you treat Marybeth like a little sister."

"No way. I'm not her brother. I'll go. I'll keep my word, but I'm not her brother."

Gerry held up his hands. "All right. I understand. That's asking too much of an adult. You must know a few eligible bachelors."

Jim nodded. "So?"

"Find one for Marybeth. Charlie thinks that's what

she needs, and if Marybeth is happy, Charlie is happy. Maybe she'll even fall in love and get married. The sooner the better."

Jim swigged down his drink. He couldn't agree more.

Charlie swept into her daughter's room. "Marybeth, thank you for agreeing to go to Gerry's place. I hoped you realized my intentions. About his son, I mean. I need to see all of us together."

Marybeth folded back the rose-colored blanket on her bed, then sat down. "I'm not sure I follow, Mom. You've seen us all together. What more do you want?"

"To see whether or not we can be a family. It will help me make a decision about my future. I won't even consider marrying Gerry unless we all get along. Being together this weekend will help me, so please don't back out."

"You two would be family, not us. Consider yourselves. We're not involved."

"You're wrong. At least for me it's wrong. I'm not a mother who turns her back on her child. Unless we all get along—I'm not saying live in each other's pockets—I won't marry Gerry."

"Do you want to marry him?"

"Yes. No. I'm not sure. I love him, that I know. It's just . . ." Her forehead puckered in a frown. "Beyond wanting to travel, he hasn't made plans for his retirement. I don't want to lose him, yet I don't want to give up my career. I want us all to be happy."

Marybeth realized she was seeing a side to her mother she'd never seen before. Her heart went out to her. For once Charline Wynston sounded nervous and uncertain. "Mom, I'm fine. Don't consider me in the equation. You've got enough on your mind, sorting out your future."

Charlie sat down on the bed next to Marybeth. "It's the way I am. I receive bundles of letters from angry relatives and upset children, regardless of age. The parent takes a new spouse, and after the first blush of love is gone, choosing up sides follows. I can deal with anything, but not that."

"That's a big responsibility you're putting on my shoulders, Mom. Mine and Jam—Jim's."

"But not too big. I'd like you two to discuss how you'd feel. I could tell you two like each other."

Marybeth stared wide-eyed at Charlie. What else could her mother tell?

Jim phoned Marybeth the following day and they arranged to see each other that evening when Gerry accompanied Charlie to a speaking engagement. Marybeth served dinner, but for all the tension she felt, she barely touched the herbed pasta, garlic bread, or Caesar salad. Jim wolfed his down.

"You wanted to go in the first place," she said accusingly, still fretting over the upcoming weekend. "You know it. You should have said you were busy."

He threw down his napkin and pushed away his plate. "I'm here to see my father. I have no reason not to go. Is the thought of spending two nights beneath the same roof with me that intolerable?"

She tried to placate him. What must he be thinking of her? She had thrown herself at him, then pushed him away. Now she laid the blame on him for their parents' invitation.

"It's not that," she said.

"Then what is it?" He refused to let her off the hook.

She threw him an annoyed look. Surely he knew why without being asked.

"Well?" he demanded.

"It's us," she said pointedly. "I don't want to start up with you again."

"Quaintly put," he said, jabbing a finger at her. "'Start up' with me. You're afraid of yourself, not me. Yesterday proved it. It's time you face facts. You want me. You're dying to *start up* with me. What's more, you're praying I'll take the choice out of your hands. That way you'll be able to convince yourself, while you beg me for more, that you were an innocent victim of my lust. No thanks. When we make love, you're coming to me as an equal. I wouldn't have it any other way."

Her heart beat faster, and she blushed. "Don't flatter yourself."

A soft oath escaped him. Exasperated, he stood and grabbed his plate, then ran the sink water full blast and washed it.

"You're splashing water on the floor!"

With a snap of his wrist the flow stopped. He wadded up some paper towels, dropped them on the floor, and stomped on them to mop the water.

"James, we are talking about our parents. We don't plan on living with them. We're not babies. What's with them? Why don't they know their own minds?"

"You don't know yours, why should they?"

"I tried," she muttered. Irked, she swept her own plate from the table. "That's a low blow. You know I'm devoting my energies to clearing my debts, to hopefully reopening for business."

There was a silence before he said, "All that energy wasted on pottery. No one can accuse you of getting off track, can they?"

"Nor you," she said, her voice choked.

He regarded her for a moment as she stood beside him, her hand clenched around the sponge, her shoulders taut. Turning from her, he pulled a business card from his wallet and grabbed a pen from the counter. After jotting down the name and phone number of a restaurant decorator, he tossed the card on the table.

"What's that?" she asked.

"You're devoting your time to clearing your debts. Give her a call." With that, he left.

Fuming, Marybeth started to rip the card. Don't be dumb! she scolded herself. A lead was a lead. She'd phone in the morning.

After cleaning the kitchen she settled in the living room and tried concentrating on a book. She couldn't. The summer reruns on television bored her.

"Come on, Peaches," she said at last to the cat. "Bedtime."

She awoke in a foul mood to a hot, humid, muggy day. When Diana invited her to lunch she was only too happy to get away from the house for a few hours.

First, though, she phoned Jim's contact.

The decorator was due back from vacation in ten days.

She checked her lottery numbers. She hadn't won.

Diana locked her store, leaving a clock sign on the door with the arrow indicating she would reopen in an hour. She'd made reservations in a nearby restaurant, and she and Marybeth walked the two blocks to the tea garden.

After they'd ordered, Marybeth filled Diana in on the latest news, telling her she'd learned of two new places that had recently opened in the area, a gallery and a furniture store. She'd visit them after lunch, show them a few items and her portfolio. "It never hurts to try. I tell myself it's the dog days of summer and not to be discouraged. If they don't need it now, maybe another day."

"You're right. What's happening with Jim?"

The memory of the kisses they'd shared, and the tension between them, clouded Marybeth's eyes. "Going away this weekend isn't a good idea. We're supposed to put on smiling faces to help my mother see us as one happy family. She's placing a lot of stock on this."

"Remember, your dad did a real number on her. She's as scared of validating her romance with Gerry as you are with Jim. As I see it, you have two choices. Yes or no. I vote you make love with Jim." She grinned. "Then you can put on a smiling face for real."

Marybeth laughed. How typical of Diana to view things as black or white. "James and I are not having a romance, and it's not that simple."

Diana raised a dubious brow. "Sure you are, and it is simple. You're making it hard. Jim is not. Seems to me he knows exactly what he wants."

"Not what," Marybeth clarified, picking up her glass of iced tea, "who. I can't get involved. If I do, I'm opening myself up for heartbreak."

"Or pleasure," Diana said, getting in the last word.

Jim stretched out his long legs and leaned back on the chaise longue in Marybeth's backyard. The sun warmed his face, and he moved out of its rays. Idling the day away was a rare occurrence for him. He had called his secretary that morning and she'd said there were no major problems, nothing he couldn't handle by phone. He'd treated his dad to lunch, then driven over to see Marybeth, purposely not calling first. The fewer opportunities he gave her to say no to him, the better.

She wasn't there, but he wasn't concerned. She had to come home sometime. Around his head he heard the low buzzing of a mosquito. As he slapped it, he heard a car turn into the driveway. Walking around to the front, he saw Marybeth behind the wheel.

Seeing him, Marybeth gritted her teeth, prepared for battle. Then he smiled. He was casually dressed in light blue trousers and a white shirt, and he looked disgustingly wonderful. She didn't trust him. As he approached, warning flags went up in her head.

She got out of the car. "James, if you've come to pick up where you left off last night, don't."

He pulled in a deep breath and expelled it slowly. It had taken him a long time to cool down the previous day, but he wasn't ready to let her out of his sight. "Fair enough. Did you phone the number I gave you?"

Carrying the vase she'd handed him from out of her car, he followed her into the air-conditioned house. She told him the woman was on vacation, then explained where she'd been that day. She placed one bowl on consignment at the gallery, and the owner of the furniture store had bought a piece for himself.

"If you're willing to sell to a decorator and to strangers," he asked, "why not to me?"

She took out two cans of sodas, popped the lids,

and poured the drinks into tall, frosted glasses. She was keenly aware of the subtly possessive way he remained close to her, and his nearness turned her insides to jelly.

"I'm not a charity case," she said. "My things aren't suitable for a fast-food chain. If they were, I'd be the first to unload them on you. The pieces would either break or be stolen, though. Pick one out for your house. It'll be my gift for your trying to help me."

"What good is it to be independent and foolish? You're ten thousand dollars in the hole. There're no medals for false pride. Have you considered applying for a loan?"

"I have no false pride. I have real pride. I'm doing what I think is right. And banks give loans only to good credit risks with collateral. I won't let my mother cosign a note. I'll work this out myself, keep on doing what I can. After Labor Day I'll look for a job."

"I offered you a job."

"You want to buy recipes. That's not a job."

Jim had to respect her will to help herself. The best he could hope for was to chip away at some of her stubborn resistance. "If custom-made pottery takes longer than mass-produced, why not mass-produce?"

"What good is it to mass-produce just for the sake of mass-producing? Where would I store it? Who's buying it? I don't want to discuss this anymore."

What she said made sense, he thought. She was five years older, five years smarter. He brushed a strand of her hair from her forehead and dropped a kiss on her cheek, startling her. "Whatever you want." He tipped up her chin. "By the way, the vases on the mantel are terrific. You're a talent. You always were. In every way, Peaches."

She gave him a wary look. "Stop kissing me. You know what that leads to. I thought we agreed to let our heads rule our actions."

He chuckled. "I never agreed to such nonsense. If I did, it was in a moment of weakness and amnesia."

"If it's amnesia, how do you remember a moment of weakness?"

"Why can't you be a little less smart?"

She smirked. "Why can't you be a little less devious?"

"I've decided to keep my options open. I was hasty once where you're concerned. I'm reforming."

"James, you don't know the meaning of the word *reform*. Can you see the two of us being thrown together for a weekend? On top of that, you offer to play sugar daddy."

"My dad wants me to find you a man. Guess why?"

Marybeth's eyes darkened until they resembled a stormy sea. "To get me out of the picture."

"Bingo. He hopes you'll marry."

She stomped past him. "Oh, he does, does he? Fine. I'll marry Dennis."

Jim muttered a curse. His first furious impulse was to drag her off by her hair, lock them both in a room, and stay there until they were old and withered. The memory of the kiss they'd shared, combined with being close to her now, breathing in her scent, had him in knots. He wanted to run his hands over her bare skin, wanted to taste her again. His father wasn't the only one mesmerized by a Wynston.

"Marry Dennis?" he repeated. "In a pig's eye you will." Threading his fingers through her thick hair, he held her head still and kissed her, increasing the pressure until she responded.

"Don't say that, even as a joke," he warned, ending the kiss but not releasing her.

She shook loose and dropped into a chair. "I bet my mother feels the same way Gerry does. I'm a fifth wheel, a boomerang baby."

He couldn't help but smile. He wouldn't mind if she boomeranged right back over to him. "What's that?"

"An adult who moves back home. Boomerang children are adults who can't make it on their own, thanks to high taxes, recession, debt, divorce, a whole bunch of reasons. Mom writes about it. It's an increasing phenomenon in our country."

"There is a a way out."

"How?"

"Come to Chicago. Work for me. I'll put you up at my apartment. Think of the money you'll save on rent."

She eyed him fishily. "I'd insist on separate bedrooms."

He wouldn't mind sleeping in her room. "Done."

"Not yet."

"Now what?"

"Double locks on the door."

He wouldn't mind locking them in. "You drive a hard bargain. Done."

She rolled her eyes upward. "Don't you ever give up?"

"No," he said, completely serious.

Six

Waiting for James to pick her up the following Saturday morning, Marybeth looked back on six days of heightening sexual tension. All week he'd shown up unexpectedly, looking incredible. He'd give her a rose, then watch her work or talk about his business. He never phoned. He simply arrived. And the more she saw him, the more she wanted to be with him.

He stole kisses when her hands were steeped in wet clay. He whispered vivid suggestions in her ear, and her fingers would slide down the cone of clay, ruining its shape. He sent jolts of simmering passion along her spine.

She loved it. But only for an interlude, she sternly reminded herself.

On Thursday she hadn't seen him until evening. He'd arrived with Gerry, who remained in the house with her mother while she and James sat in the backyard.

James had pulled her to him and given her a warm, thorough kiss, then studied her closely. "You're edgy. Necking like a pair of high school kids isn't enough for us."

She pushed him away. "I am not edgy." She had passed edgy on Monday, uptight on Tuesday, fidgety on Wednesday, and now was ready to crawl the walls.

"I'm edgy," he murmured, trailing his lips along her cheek. "You're going to have to help me out. I'm in bad shape." She gasped as his hand cupped her breast. "Sweetheart, if I don't make love to you soon, I'm going to explode."

"No," she said. "You'll be leaving soon and we'll both resume our normal lives." She was determined to guard her heart, to stay the course. Still, she marveled that she spoke the words so calmly. With his arms around her, her whole body responded to his slightest touch. He was right. She was addicted to him. Physically, at least.

Again, he urged her either to sell him her recipes or develop new ones for him in her own kitchen. "I'll put you under contract," he said. "Promise me you'll think about it."

She promised.

On Friday he accompanied her to Diana's. They fell into their old friendship with ease, and he shamelessly enlisted her aid. "Tell Peaches to sell me her inventory."

"Sell it to him," Diana said. "His money's as good as anyone else's."

She told them both where to get off. Later she spoke with him alone, reiterating that she didn't need handouts. That started a shouting match.

"You're pigheaded and stubborn!" he yelled.

"Call me whatever you please. I refuse to be beholden to you."

"But you're willing to be beholden to a stranger?"

"Oh, for goodness' sakes! Selling my inventory to someone who can use it isn't the same thing."

"It's impossible to talk sense into you!"

"Fine! Next week you can return to Chicago with the comfort of knowing I'm brainless. In the meantime, you'll do me a big favor by not offering to buy a load of pottery you can't use. Don't tell me you're opening a store."

After he stormed out of the house, she got a call from one of the magazines she'd sent her portfolio to. The art director complimented her work and asked if he could retain the pictures for possible future use. She'd agreed gladly.

Now, as the doorbell rang, she rushed to answer it. She'd dressed for the trip in red shorts and a T-shirt, her hair styled in a single thick braid.

James whistled when he saw her. He was all smiles, a peace offering of a single peach-colored rose in his hand. "Nice," he said, his gaze roaming leisurely over her body.

Accepting the rose and all it implied, she gave in to the pleasure of seeing him. He was dressed in cut-offs, and a well-worn blue sweatshirt. Her eyes softened in recognition. "You still wear it."

He grinned. It was the last present he'd received from her. "It's comfortable. It fits like a glove."

"Oh." He'd said that about them once too.

He loaded her picnic hamper filled with vegetable dips, cold pasta salads, and iced tea in the car.

"Who's caring for the cat?" he asked as they started off.

"My neighbor looks in on her."

"What do you know about fishing?"

"Nothing. When I want fish, I buy it. I refuse to bait a hook."

He smiled. "Worms don't cry."

"Says who?"

"All right, we won't fish. Did you bring your swimsuit?"

"No," she lied.

"Even better. We'll swim naked."

"James, turn this car around."

He speeded up, grinning at her. "Peaches, I know where we can be alone. It's a paradise within a paradise. You'll be perfectly safe from prying eyes."

"Except yours."

"Except mine. Mine will devour you."

"No, thanks."

He laughed. "Let's enjoy the weekend. Do you remember the things we did to each other? How we made each other feel? How and where I kissed you? How and where you kissed me? We knew each other completely."

She did remember, and his words evoked a heat she remembered too.

In a good mood, he began to hum along with the radio. Marybeth shook her head. There was no sense in pretending she didn't enjoy his company. For the rest of the trip they kept up a lighthearted conversation, talking about a variety of things, but never themselves.

"How much longer?" she asked when they exited the thruway in the lake area of the Catskills.

"Not far," James said. He pointed to the Trading Post, the local general store where people shopped and caught up on the latest gossip. He showed her the town's tiny business district, consisting of a post office, gas station, and several restaurants that served good, plain food.

"We're almost there."

As they drove out of town they passed large houses set back from the country road, many with the wide wraparound porches Marybeth loved. Most homes had vegetable gardens. Corn grew high in the fields. Along the way, they passed walkers and people riding bicycles. At the half-mile mark, Jim turned left, entering the secluded property by passing slowly through tall, scrolled iron gates.

"Here we are."

Marybeth sat up tall to get her first glimpse of a stretch of fields and trees. Grass and daisies spouted from the center of the winding gravel road. It descended in a wide curve, edged by a border of wintergreen bushes and sapling pines. At its base lay a shimmering lake, nestled in a necklace of rhododendron, mountain laurel, and thickets of trees. A strip of land partially bisected the lake, creating on one side a giant swimming pool, its banks lushly green and dotted with daisies and thistles. She gazed at the trees rising majestically to the mountain's summit on the far side of the lake.

"James, it's beautiful. It's paradise."

He was thinking that paradise was anywhere she was. He stopped the car near a clump of blue-eyed grass, their tiny flowers ruffling in the soft wind. With his face near hers, he pointed to a cluster of huckleberry bushes. "Your favorite. Listen."

She did. To water splashing over the dam, carrying the spring-fed lake's excess water downstream. To birds chattering, to chipmunks and squirrels chasing through leaves. To bullfrogs.

"You should hear the frogs at night," he said.

"Oh, why is that?" she asked.

He gave her a smoldering look. "That's when they show off their mating calls." The gleam in his eye had her drawing a quick breath. He stroked her hair, her face. The warmth from his touch made her tremble.

"James, please . . ."

He touched her lips gently with his fingertips. "There's the house."

He pointed, and she saw the white clapboard house that sat on a small rise overlooking the lake. It had a wide porch. On it was a hammock on a metal stand, white and blue wicker rockers and chairs, and pots of red and white geraniums. A redwood table and chairs, shaded by a permanent roof, were set on a concrete slab near the lake's floating dock. The dock, with attached benches and room for more chairs, was protected from the sun's rays by an enormous yellow and white fringed umbrella.

To get a better look, she leaned across him, bracing her hand on his thigh. Her breast pressed against his chest.

"Marybeth."

She tipped her face up to his. Their gazes locked. The outside world retreated as memories of intimate moments flooded their minds. Each swallowed hard. Marybeth's heart pounded.

"Shouldn't we go?" she asked.

"In a minute. Right now I would appreciate it very much if you would get out of the damned car so I can kiss you properly."

She could no more stop herself from obeying than she could stop her heart from banging against the wall of her chest. He took her hand and led her to a secluded area, out of sight of the road and house.

Memories of the intimacies they had shared fueled her craving and chipped away at her resistance. Some of the reasons that had driven them apart years before still existed. But her need for his touch overwhelmed her better sense.

His hands glided over her rib cage and settled on her hips. "We said we'd enjoy the weekend. For once in your life, stop figuring the odds. Kiss me. Let yourself feel."

She did. With a small groan she crushed her mouth to his. Her body fit unerringly to his, recharged and starving for more. She wound her arms around his neck, leaning into him, feeling his hard chest, his rapidly beating heart.

Bodies fused in the taking.

Lips possessed in the giving.

Time stood still.

Stopped.

And finally restarted.

He released her, but only after giving her another kiss that made her head spin. "Keeping my hands off you in front of our parents isn't going to be easy."

Opening her eyes slowly, she pressed her hands against his chest. "These aren't the old days. We live in different states. You have your priorities, I have mine. And it would be unfair of us to complicate our parents' lives right now."

"You're right," he said tersely as they walked back to the car. "But I don't have to like it."

From around a bend in the lake they spotted Gerry rowing the boat, Charlie resting against a cushion.

"Stay out on the lake," James shouted. "We'll join you in a few minutes."

The house was everything Charlie had said. The spacious country interior lent a feeling of instant welcome, of peace and well-being. Large, with open, beamed ceilings, the great room had dual sofas that invited comfort, an intimate grouping of chairs that begged conversation, and a card table and television set that offered entertainment. Quarry stone framed a large fireplace. The sunny yellow kitchen, equipped with modern appliances, overlooked the lake, as did the dining area with its oak table that sat eight. The floors were polished oak, left bare except for occasional rugs. One wall held a serigraph Jim had given his father.

He led her to the master bedroom, located in one wing of the house. "It's beautiful," she said, lightly running her fingers over the pine furniture.

"Come on, I'll show you where you'll sleep."

They retraced their steps to the other side of the house. Jim walked into his bedroom, then opened a door and strolled into hers. The room was furnished with a double bed and a dresser. An afghan was neatly draped over the back of a wing chair near the window, and on the pine nightstand was a milk bottle with a bouquet of daisies and thistles.

He grinned at her. "This is convenient, don't you think?"

Too convenient, she thought. "I think I'm going to buy you a chastity belt."

They went outside and watched as Gerry rowed to shore. He dropped anchor, then helped Charlie out of the boat. Gerry hugged Marybeth as Jim said hello to her mother.

"This is terrific!" Gerry said. "We've planned a cookout for tonight. Charlie's already made a salad. Jim, you're a master chef. I'll let you do the honors at the grill."

Their parents were so full of enthusiasm, so happy to see them, they made it easy to be a foursome, to catch their infectious mood.

"Marybeth made pasta salad," Jim said, then added loyally, "I tasted it. It's delicious."

She sent him a grateful smile of appreciation, then ruined it by offering to cook veggie burgers for Gerry and Charlie.

"We prefer steak, thank you," Gerry said.

After they'd carried Jim's and Marybeth's bags in, they settled on the shady porch. Jim and Gerry filled Charlie and Marybeth in on the neighbors, who lived where and for how long. The community boasted generations of families. Some lived there permanently, others used their homes strictly for vacations.

"It beats city living any day," Gerry said.

"Wouldn't you feel isolated here year round?" Charlie asked.

"Would you?"

"Don't be a psychiatrist, Gerry. I asked first."

He leaned back in his chair, resting his feet on a tree stump he'd fashioned for a footrest. "I think I'd like to try it. I've thought about it often. When the solitude got to me, I'd travel. Your turn, Charlie."

"Not having spent much time here, I can only guess what it would be like. Part of me is a city girl, though. I enjoy art exhibits, going to the theater, restaurants, that sort of thing. There's an excitement in the city that you can't get anyplace else. It rubs off on you. Also, I need to be near an airport for when I travel to give lectures."

Marybeth exchanged glances with Jim.

Gerry sat forward, his expression serious. "We're not exactly at the end of the world here. You can drive to the city in less than a couple of hours. There's a bus, too, or you could even hire a car."

Charlie patted his hand. "You've got your priorities straight. I can learn a lesson from you."

Gerry beamed. "Isn't she wonderful?"

Jim wished Marybeth had been that easy to convince five years before. But with his dad's plans still up in the air, Charlie had spoken hypothetically. In his own case, he had tried to force Marybeth into an immediate decision, one she hadn't been ready to make.

Dinner was a gab and food fest. They ate outside. Everyone agreed that Jim barbecued the best-tasting rib-eye steak, Charlie made the best tomato and mixed greens salad, Marybeth the best pasta salad with chives, peas, red peppers, and spices. Gerry was dubbed the best all-around eater. They remained outside until a fine mist forced them inside. Gerry kept an assortment of games, and they opted for cards, the women teamed against the men. They played a fast, hilarious game of gin rummy, craning necks to sneak looks at cards slapped down on shifting piles.

"You're cheating!" Jim accused Marybeth at one point, clamping a hand around her wrist. She held the ace of spades. "You stole it!"

Her eyes twinkled. "Me? How can you say that?"

He grinned. "I know you. Put it back."

"Oh, pooh!" She laughed. "The trouble with you, James, is that you've got a memory like an elephant! Here's your stupid card. But if I can't cheat, I won't play."

He ruffled her hair. "Naturally. What else is new?"

The game ended with the men winning.

"I'm going for a walk," Marybeth said. She slipped on her Windbreaker and jammed a hat onto her head.

"Just a minute." Jim rose. "I'll go with you. It's dark out there, and you don't know your way around." He grabbed a flashlight, his own jacket, and left with her.

The bullfrogs were out in force, bellowing and croaking.

"Great night for love, that one just said," Marybeth translated.

"It could be for us too," Jim replied, cupping her chin in his hand.

"Not under your father's roof."

"Then we'll sleep outside."

Refusing to give in to the pleasure of agreeing, of throwing herself into his arms, she said she was looking forward to a good night's sleep. He sighed deeply. They finished their walk with an unfulfilled desire, a ticking time bomb waiting for release.

Marybeth was careful to retire first, saying her good-nights while the others chatted over cups of hot chocolate. Taking her nightgown with her, she went into the bathroom to shower, then brush her hair and teeth. At last she came out of the steamy room—and walked straight into a barechested Jim.

They stood motionless in the hall, both hesitating to move apart, both yearning to step forward. In the past they would have melded naturally into each other's arms.

"If you need anything, call," he said huskily.

She slid her gaze upward, past his bronzed muscled chest to his eyes. "I will."

He caressed her cheek. "Is there a reason a friend can't kiss a friend good night?"

"No," she whispered, lifting her face. He slid his arms around her and kissed her passionately. It left them both wanting more.

"This is nuts," he muttered. "College dorms are coed."

"This isn't a dorm. Remember, our parents deserve a shot at happiness. It's just that nothing has changed with us. Our bodies still react the way they always did."

He grunted. "Charged and ready."

"Not here."

"Dammit, I'm not trying to win a medal for good behavior." He yanked her to him, cupping her buttocks and proving with hard accuracy how much he wanted her. She gave in to the pleasure of his reaction, then sighed and eased out of his embrace.

He gripped her arm. "Take the thought of me holding you naked in my arms to bed."

Marybeth fled to her room. She reminded herself he'd be returning to Chicago. She didn't need to compound her problems by adding emotional turmoil to financial woes. Any person with half a brain knew piling stress upon stress solved nothing.

She drowned out the sentence James had told her to think about. How could she sleep thinking about lying naked in his arms?

Guard your heart, she told herself sternly. These weren't the old days. Five years before, she'd hurt him as deeply as he'd hurt her. For all she knew he wanted to make love to her simply to prove he could still make her burn. She resisted the impulse to charge into his room and tell him he could. He didn't have to prove it. Her sermon completed, she punched the pillow and slammed down her head.

And stared at the darkened ceiling.

She could use a massage to relieve the tension in her neck. James had given her her first massage. She'd been cramming for midterm exams, burning the lights far into the night for over a week, ignoring her exhaustion and nervous tension. James had finally had enough, and grabbed her book from her.

"You're on overload," he said. He refused to give her the book back when she said she had to study more for the morning exam. "You're doing yourself no good."

He spread thick terry-cloth towels on the kitchen table, then, using scented oils and working from the tip of her toes to her neck, he massaged her sore muscles. When she was completely relaxed, he led her to the shower, stepping in with her. As the soothing warm water sprayed over them, he started kissing and caressing her in a totally different way. Later, he wrapped her in towels, carried her to bed, and made slow, languorous love to her. The next day she aced the test.

And now, she thought, the great masseur slept on the other side of a thin wall.

Outside, stars blanketed the sky. Fireflies sent out phosphorescent sparks of light; frogs, bullfrogs, and crickets kept up a steady racket. She leaned up on her elbow to gaze out the window. Mist hovered over the lake in a silvery-gray blanket.

Still restless at midnight, she snapped on the light to read a book, and she noticed a band of light peeping beneath the door to James's room. At one A.M. she turned off the light. At one-thirty James switched off his lamp. At three she used the bathroom.

Wide awake in his bed, James restrained himself from charging through the connecting doors to her bedroom. At five he prowled to the bathroom. At five-thirty he stalked around his room.

Wide awake in her room, Marybeth threw the covers over her head in a useless attempt to drown out his footsteps. She forced herself to stay there when all she wanted was to feed on his warmth.

By dawn the mist over the lake was dancing upward in graceful spirals. The rowboat rocked gently at the dock, its oars tucked inside the boat, waiting. At six A.M. both Jim and Marybeth were staring at the ceiling, yawning and cursing the common wall.

On the other side of the house in the master bedroom, Charlie and Gerry slept like babies, in their favorite spoon position. They rose early, refreshed from a good night's sleep. They kissed, hopped out of bed, showered, and dressed. Charlie started breakfast for Gerry, who, like herself, was a morning person.

At 6:30 Jim, moving like a zombie, got out of bed, dressed, and washed.

At 6:45 Marybeth nodded to him in the hall outside the bathroom. He pulled her to him abruptly. His sleepy gaze sped her heartbeat. His unspoken message—*this has to stop*—there for her to read.

She washed, pulled on a fuschia-colored cotton top and blue jeans, and dragged herself into the kitchen. On the table was a bowl of fresh berries and several boxes of cereals. A pitcher of orange juice sat on the counter. The aroma of brewed coffee filled the room. Jim was slouched in a chair.

"How did you sleep?" Gerry asked Marybeth. He wore frayed cutoffs, a T-shirt, and sneakers.

Her heavy eyelids, her sluggish limbs, and her heart felt like dead weights. She muffled a yawn.

"Terrific." Taking a glass, she filled it a third of the way with water, then added juice. Yawning, she handed the glass to Jim.

Gerry observed the silent exchange. "How did you sleep, Jim?"

He rubbed his chin. "Fine, Pop, fine. Aren't you having juice, Marybeth?"

"You know it's too early for me." She yawned, blinked. "I'm going outside for a walk. I can't imagine why I'm so tired."

Charlie stopped whisking eggs. "You're relaxing, darling. You too, Jim. You both need another good night's rest like you had last night. By tomorrow morning you'll feel wonderful. I firmly believe the body craves what it needs."

Jim caught Marybeth's eye. She looked away and strode outside.

After Marybeth had gone, Charlie offered to fix Jim's breakfast. He declined, saying he'd grab something later, then he left too.

"What was that all about?" Gerry asked as Charlie set his plate before him. "The excuse you gave them is a bunch of hogwash. If anything, mountain air gives you such a good night's sleep, you wake up refreshed."

Charlie stared out the window. After a moment she shook her head, as if discounting a thought. "Marybeth's sleeping in a strange bed. I don't know Jim's sleeping habits, but when two people come down with the same malady, I'd say it's likely the strange beds."

Gerry bit into a buttered roll. "It doesn't bother you. You sleep like a log."

Charlie kissed his cheek, then snatched a piece of his bacon. "I have you, you old goat. Of course I sleep well. You knock me out."

Looking very smug, he swatted her rump. "Watch who you call an old goat."

"Old coot!" she teased.

"You're right!" he whooped. "I'm glad Jim's paying attention to your daughter. It gives us time alone."

Smiling, her eyes shining, Charlie sat down to join him for breakfast. "My thoughts exactly."

Cursing, Jim kicked a stone aside as he climbed a winding path. Turmoil settled in his gut. No woman in the world could tie him in knots the way Marybeth did just by sleeping in the next room. At the rate he was going, he'd never win her back. One minute he was the cool adult, the next a callow jerk!

He walked for a half hour, then switched course, seeking Marybeth. He found her quickly. She had wandered onto the spit of land that bisected a portion of the lake. Her thumbs hooked into the loops of her jeans, she was peering into the lake.

"Hello," he said.

"Shh. I'm counting fish." A school of minnows swam by followed by a long-snout bullet-shape pickerel.

"Beats counting sheep."

She cocked her head to look at him. "You didn't sleep either?"

"How could I with you tossing around on the other side of the wall? I wanted to crawl into bed with you, kiss off that thin nightgown, and make love to you. Then we'd both get some rest. You heard your mom. The body craves what it needs. Mine's craving. I am not in a good mood."

"She shook her head. "Don't you dare blame me. I didn't want to come in the first place."

"Great. Blame me. Did it ever occur to you this whole thing is a crazy case of role reversal? We're worrying like parents do about our children's happiness, afraid to do anything for ourselves."

"Not under your father's roof," she said adamantly.

Jim wondered if she realized that with her reply, she'd just tactily admitted they were going to make love. "I shouldn't complain," he said, "not when I can see my dad so happy. Once I heard him cry. He doesn't know. It was right after he and my mom had sat me down to tell me they were divorcing. He braved it out, then left the room to go to their bedroom. I've never seen him so forlorn, so despairing. I was in shock too. My mother left the house. I went to talk to dad, but when I neared the bedroom I heard him crying. I couldn't bring myself to intrude on his privacy."

They returned to the house, and Jim accepted Gerry's offer to go fishing. Marybeth and Charlie drove to town.

Gerry rowed to the far side of the lake while Jim baited the hooks. They dropped their lines, then Jim closed his eyes, lulled by the gentle movement of the boat. Gerry started to talk, but within minutes he was speaking to himself. Jim snored lightly, his chin resting on his chest.

When he awoke an hour later, he blinked and grinned. "What were you saying, Pop?"

"You're quite a fisherman, Jim. In your sleep you caught two bass and a sunny." Gerry lifted the fishing pail from the water to show the fish in the bucket.

"What did you catch?" Jim asked as he cast his line.

"Nothing. I was too busy catching yours. Do you think Marybeth's having a good time?"

Jim saw the anxious look on his dad's face. "I'm sure of it, Pop."

Gerry smiled. He rowed to another spot, then brought the paddles into the boat, dropped anchor, and cast his line. "I'm glad. Charlie likes you, Jim."

"I like her too. Does this mean wedding bells will be ringing?"

"I hope so. The time's pretty close now. I had my dream set on traveling, maybe living here. Despite what Charlie said last night about me knowing my priorities, she won't be happy living my dream. Thing is, I can't see myself sitting around doing nothing while she works. Or worse, being Mr. Henrietta Heartfelt."

Jim nodded. He saw a glimmer of possible trouble looming on the horizon. "To quote a wise cop I know, if you love each other, you'll work it out."

"Tell the truth, Jim, I'm reluctant to broach the subject. I suppose it's cowardly on my part."

"Not at all," Jim argued. "You've known each other a short time. You can't solve everything in one day."

"Charlie's not interested in retiring. In case you haven't noticed, she's a very independent lady."

Like mother, like daughter, Jim thought.

"What should I do, Jim?"

"Dad, whatever you decide, don't let her go."

"Who said anything about letting her go? I'm not crazy. She means everything to me. I want to do this right. To make sure that one day she and I will marry. I don't want a repeat of the past when unfinished business got in the way. That's the main reason your mother's and my marriage broke up."

"What are you saying?"

"My occupation isn't all that dangerous. As a composite artist, my work starts after the gunplay. Still, the uniform, badge, and gun didn't help, I admit. Your mom's a good woman. I'm glad she finally found a man who helped her through her unfinished business."

Jim nodded. He liked his mother's new husband, whom she'd married when Jim was twenty-two. "What do you mean by unfinished business, Pop?"

"The unresolved stuff we carry with us, often, not always, from childhood. You remember your mom's mother? She was your mom's unfinished business."

Jim had a vague recollection of a stern grandmother whose smile didn't reach her eyes. When he visited her spotless home, the filled candy dish sat untouched. His mother had warned him never to take candy unless offered.

"She was the strictest person I knew. I hated going there."

"Can you imagine what it must have been like for

your mother in that house? Whenever your mother and I argued, I couldn't get past her barriers, past the child in her crying out. I failed her."

"Don't blame yourself," Jim said quickly. Regardless of what had happened between his mother and Gerry, the abundance of love Gerry had showered on him shaped him into the man he was today. He was fortunate.

Gerry reeled in his line, then stood and flicked his wrist, casting the line far out. The boat rocked as he sat down. "Don't get me wrong. Not all problems are rooted in childhood, despite what a bunch of psychologists write in books and yak about on television. We adults make mistakes as adults. The trick is not to repeat them, to learn from the previous error."

"You're a wise man, Pop."

He shrugged. "Thanks. I'm trying. One of these days, Jim, you'll fall in love. You never went into detail about the woman you loved years ago. I'm not asking now. That's water under the bridge. None of us can go backward. When a certain woman comes along, a woman who gets under your skin, a woman you can't let go, you'll know what I mean. Trust me, you'll know what need is."

His father had just defined his feelings for Marybeth, Jim mused. Seeing her the previous evening in her nightgown and seeing her again that morning in the hall, looking sleepy and wonderful, her hair disheveled, her eyes drowsy, had raised his body heat. When he held her she was soft and warm, her scent alluring. No, nothing had changed in five years—except for added complications.

He reeled in his line. "Sounds to me as if you've answered your own question, Pop. You know what to do. Find a new dream with Charlie."

Gerry's attention was caught by the sound of tires on gravel. Looking up, they saw Gerry's car pull up by the house. Charlie and Marybeth were back. Gerry pulled up anchor.

"Thanks for listening," he said. "You're right, of course. Now, if you don't mind, let's row back to the ladies. I'd like to talk with Charlie. Is there something you can think of to do with Marybeth for a few hours?"

Technically, Jim thought, they wouldn't be under his father's roof. He smiled. His pulses stirred. "I think I can find a way to occupy her time."

Seven

"Where are we going?" Marybeth asked as Jim drove off in a cloud of dust, leaving Gerry and Charlie to put away the groceries. The moment he and Gerry had climbed out of the boat, Jim announced he was taking Marybeth sight-seeing.

Gerry waved them off. "Enjoy yourselves. Don't hurry back."

"What's this all about?" Marybeth asked as Jim helped her into his car. "If I didn't know better, I'd think you and Gerry were in cahoots to get me out of the house."

"We are. Dad needs to speak with your mom. Alone."

Now, as Jim turned onto a road that wasn't much bigger than a path, she asked again, "Where are we going?"

"To keep a rendezvous away from prying eyes." He let the implications of his statement hang in the air. Driving slowly, he inched the car deeper into a forest. The canopy of trees swallowed them up.

"This is as far as we can take the car," he said at last.

Carrying a blanket he'd snagged from the porch, he took her hand and led her into the forest. The earth was soft, layered in places with leaves, in other places cushioned by moss or a carpet of pine needles. The scent of pine perfumed the air. Cottony clouds appeared to hang in the azure sky. Robins, cardinals, and bluejays jabbered at them. Then a different sound caught her attention.

"What do I hear?" she asked.

"The waterfalls. We're almost there."

They came to an area of tall grass dotted with yellow daisies, purple thistles, cardinal flowers, and flag iris. Jim plucked a daisy and tucked it behind Marybeth's ear. He kissed her palm, then cupped her face in his hands, gazing deeply into her eyes.

"For five years," he said in a voice raw with emotion, "I've imagined us making love. I admit it was usually in a bed, but this is better. We're under God's roof, not man's. Now's the time to back out, not later. If I touch you, I won't stop."

She was motionless for a moment, staring at him, then she nodded. "I won't let you stop."

She leaned into him, fitting herself against his lean, hard body. Her hands around his neck, she smiled brightly into his eyes, her lashes glistening with tears. "Last night when I heard you tossing in your bed, I knew you were hurting too. I wanted to take you into me and love you."

"No more waiting."

Sinking to their knees, they shed unwanted clothing. He gazed in wonder at the glowing green-eyed goddess of his memory. Summer glistened in her hair. Her full, ripe lips beckoned to be kissed, her breasts begged for his touch. Seeing her, his hunger was unleashed.

The first electric contact of flesh upon flesh had

them clinging to each other, sighing with pleasure. She tucked her cheek into his shoulder. His fingers combed through her shiny chestnut hair, sifting the shimmering strands. He buried his face in it to breathe in its clean scent.

"Let me look at you," he said, easing her away, his hand gliding over the curve of her hip.

She felt shy all of a sudden. The emotion surprised her. He had seen her naked many times. They had spent nights locked in each other's arms, limbs entwined as if they couldn't stand even the slightest separation. He was the only man she'd ever loved, yet she felt as if this were their first time.

He studied her in quiet contemplation. "Have I changed?" she asked.

He understood her question. In truth, he'd been wondering how she would receive him. That she worried about his reaction endeared her to him more. His gaze swept appreciatively over her curvaceous figure. His arms tightened around her.

"You're more beautiful, more lovely than I remembered."

She smiled, and her arms went around his strong shoulders, relearning his taut muscles. He was magnificently built. She couldn't resist running the tips of her fingers down the length of his body. She heard him gasp. For a heart-stopping moment their gazes spoke of raw desire.

Then he lowered his head.

His mouth captured hers. Ignited by fires that could burn only for him, she returned his kiss. He resisted the impulse to take her then, to bury himself inside her, to sheath himself in her welcoming warmth. He kissed first one, then the other breast, tugging gently on her nipples, rolling his tongue on the hardening tips. Fanning her passions, he trailed heated kisses down her belly to nuzzle the juncture of her thighs.

Marybeth felt her heart leap into her throat. Her body responded to the sweet agony, the throbbing, aching, insatiable need for more. He led her to a pleasure-driven world, a private garden, a sensual paradise inhabited only by them. She molded herself to him, her hips circling in a restless cadence. He tortured her with exquisite pain, alternating between kissing and fondling the nub of nerves at her center, masterfully creating a spiral of ever-tightening carnal coils.

Her fingers clutched the blanket. Poised on the brink, helpless to stop, she bucked upward in a blinding flash. As she shattered in thousands of tiny nerve cells, she shouted his name, delighting him with her cry.

A surge of pride engulfed him. He whispered words of loving celebration. After five years she belonged to him now more than ever. Gathering her in his arms, he held her until her breathing evened. "Thank you," he murmured.

Marybeth lifted her index finger and slowly traced the outline of his mouth. She rained kisses on his lips, his cheeks, his chin, his neck. Her eyes aglow with anticipation, she pushed him flat on his back. "It's only fair."

A natural temptress, she embarked on an intimate journey, using him for her roadmap. He moaned deeply, his greedy body accepting her kisses, responding to how she was fondling him, pleasuring him in still-remembered lessons.

She plunged her tongue into his mouth, mating with his, her hair forming a chestnut cloud around them, a curtain of privacy. She closed her hand over him, stoking the fire in his loins. Stretching over him like a soft, lazy kitten, she seduced him to the point of helpless need.

He grasped her hips, a harsh plea escaping him. "Stop."

"No."

"Witch."

Her husky laugh ran out.

"Peaches," he groaned. "You're going to have to stop. Now."

She gazed into his smoldering eyes. Hers darkened. In seconds he shifted, changing their positions, wrapping her legs around his back. He braced himself on his elbows, poised above her.

"You are the most intoxicating perfume in this forest."

Even before he completed his sentence, he joined his body to hers. Covering her muffled cries with his mouth, he began to move inside her. She rose up to meet him, pulling him deeper, closer, tighter, striving to give him the release he sought.

He thrust in and out, surging on a fast tide. His breath quickened as her moans of ecstasy urged him on. All of her cried out to him. Thrusting harder, faster, aroused by her scent, by the soft swelling of her belly meeting the hard flat planes of his, he gave in to the sweet madness. He reveled in her femininity, that his manhood could give her such pleasure.

With a guttural cry he poured his love into her, giving her all of him. In return he captured all of her.

Afterward, he held her fiercely to his chest, never wanting to let her go, silently swearing to keep her with him at all costs. When their ragged breathing slowed and steadied, he tilted her face upward and smiled into her eyes. They were meant to be. He would do whatever was necessary to ensure they never part again.

The afternoon sun fanned by a warm breeze dried their bodies. From their bed in the clearing, neither made a move to rise. Around and above them birds serenaded them. Jim leaned over and lightly brushed his lips across her forehead. They laced their fingers together, letting the time stretch out.

"We're good together," he said.

"The best," she answered, relaxed.

He lifted her hand, then let it drop on his chest. "Would you do something for me?"

She looked curious. "What?"

"Let me help you?"

She rose on one elbow. "You have the longest eyelashes."

"So do you. Answer the question."

"I told you. I'm working on it." She snuggled in his arms, refusing to spoil the day with thoughts of business. Right now she felt happy, complete. She resolutely pushed aside the unpleasant thought that he would be leaving soon. Today was theirs, their gift to each other, their blessing. She would allow nothing to dampen her spirits.

He patted her rump and sighed. For now he tabled the discussion, fully intending to bring it up again. "Let's go. But put on a minimum of clothes. You'll just be taking them off soon."

"Where to now?"

"The day won't be complete unless we swim in the pool the beavers built."

They dressed. Taking her hand, Jim led the way. Their crunching steps disturbed squirrels and birds. The trail twisted so much, Marybeth thought they were going in circles until Jim parted a tangle of low-hanging vines. He held them back for them to pass through, then dropped them again. She felt as if the forest had closed behind them. The sounds were sharper, louder, the air cooler. He guided her down a rock-strewn path to a clearing.

She uttered a squeal of delight. He had brought her to a flowered Garden of Eden, an idyllic setting for the small pool. Fed by waterfalls that splashed over a rocky ledge, the water sparkled in the sun.

Awestruck, she asked, "How did you find this?"

He threw his arms around her shoulders. "When I was a kid I used to explore. Beavers dammed up the opposite ends. Those fallen logs also trapped the water, forming a basin."

They stripped quickly, then ran into the water with arms wide, making a great splash. The first shock had her teeth chattering. She swam vigorously, quickly growing accustomed to the temperature. An excellent swimmer, Jim cut through the water, his body like a sleek seal's.

After a while she flipped over onto her back, lazy and content to float. Jim treaded water beside her. He watched her avidly, her face in profile, her breasts jutting skyward, her hair streaming out on the surface of the water. Lord, he loved her.

She glanced over at him, her eyes radiant. "I could do this all day."

He snagged her waist, pulling her to shallow water. Cupping her head with one hand and supporting her back with his other arm, he kissed her with a deep hunger, his urgent message unmistakably clear.

She answered his silent question. "Yes," she whispered, caressing his face. Taking his hand, she followed him out of the water.

Marybeth cracked open an eye. Jim snored softly at her side. Leaning over, she shook his shoulder.

"We should dress before our folks send out a search party."

He stretched and ran a hand down her back. "Spoilsport. I was hoping for a massage." He rolled to a sitting position and got up. They dressed quickly.

"Did your mother indicate where things stand between her and my dad?" Jim asked, folding the blanket.

"No more than she's said before."

He tucked the blanket under his arm and led the way back toward the car. "If I were Dad, I'd have planned ahead for my retirement. He didn't. He says when he retires, he's going to loaf, travel, not think about tomorrow."

"What can we do?"

"Nothing. That's a problem for them to solve. Let's discuss us, Peaches." He grabbed her hand, forcing her to walk alongside him. "Now more than ever, I want you to let me help you. Give me recipes to send to my people in Chicago. My cooking staff will know which are practical for mass production, which aren't."

She pretended to be fascinated by the antics of a chipmunk when all she could think of was his leaving.

"James, you're being kind. The fact is—the truth is—you don't need the recipes any more than you need the pottery. Face it, you want me, but you don't need me."

His eyes blazed with irritation. "Never say that to me again, dammit. What was this afternoon? A meaningless roll in the hay? Kindness? In my book, it was need. Do you honestly believe we're not going to make love again? As often as possible? We have a past. It worked for us today. We proved again we want each other. If you think you can go on without me now, I'll show you what a liar you are. Right here. What's more, I'm willing to bet you'll help."

She tugged her hand free. "You don't fight fair."

He flailed out, forgetting his promise to himself to remain calm. "You set dumb rules, then expect me to agree to them."

"What happened to your free will?"

"What free will?" he stormed. "Where you're concerned, I'd do anything to keep you."

"I suppose I should be flattered. But I refuse to threaten my mother's chance at happiness."

His voice rang through the trees. "Who said anything about making her unhappy? I'm as concerned about my father as you are about your mother. But they have nothing to do with us."

"You don't honestly believe that. Even if you were right, I have debts to pay off, obligations to meet."

The stubbornness she confused with independence drove him crazy. "Will you let me pay your debts?"

"Thank you, but no. If I wouldn't take money from my mother, I certainly wouldn't accept it from you."

"Consider it a loan."

"With what collateral? Me? I'm not selling myself. Today was free, you know."

He struggled to maintain his composure, but failed utterly and ended up cursing. Liberally. His voice crackled with disgust.

"Thanks for the insult. You have the most marvelous way of twisting my meaning." He strode past her, then whirled in his tracks.

"All right," he said. "We'll wait. Until you pay off your debts. Until you sell all the pottery. Until our parents make a decision. Until we throw them a wedding party. Until they celebrate their fiftieth wedding anniversary! Until I'm too old to make love to you! Will you be satisfied then, you stubborn woman?"

She steamed forward, crunching pine needles beneath her feet. In a gesture of defiant indifference, she chucked him under the chin. "That will be the day!" she tossed over her shoulder, then marched to the car and hurled herself into the seat.

It took him a few seconds to realize she had fired off a compliment.

He got into a car, choking back his laughter. His knuckles caressed her cheek. "You haven't changed one bit. You still drive me crazy. Don't expect me to sleep alone tonight, Peaches."

"Not in your father's house, James. I mean it."

"Then we'll sleep outside in a sleeping bag."

She shook her head. "Not me. I'm not the camping type. I'm afraid of bugs and creepy crawlies."

He slapped the steering wheel. "Do you realize our parents will get a good night's sleep and not us? I want you with me. Don't say no."

She kissed his angry mouth. He would never change. He was an incredibly impatient, sexy man. "Just like that? What do I tell my mother? Or your father?"

He scowled. "The truth. It's time they knew. If not, we'll tell them you've made a practical decision. You're coming to work for me."

"Jim, all that talk about testing recipes from my house was baloney. You were just trying to get me to go to Chicago to sleep with me. You don't need that excuse anymore. I know it and you know it."

"I'm serious, dammit! It could work. You'd be applying your other talent, cooking, for financial reward. Millions of people switch careers. Tell our parents I offered you a job and that you accepted. From now on your nights will be taken up with on-the-job training. Do you have a problem with that?"

She did. "In the first place, no one works all night. In the second place, Mom knows I'm not a fast-food junkie."

"Listen, we are no good apart. Tell her I'm opening a pasta bar for the health-conscious customers."

"But that's not decided yet."

He cursed. "It is now! Tell her you're helping me get it started. That way we can spend time together. How else can we be alone?"

"What's the name of this business?"

"How the hell should I know? I'm for the truth about us."

"No, I won't complicate their lives."

He eased the car around a boulder and struck a rut instead. He jerked the car back onto the trail. "Call it Peaches' Pasta!" he yelled. "And either you say yes or I tell them about us."

"Are you blackmailing me?" she yelled back.

"Damn right I am. What's your answer?"

"Peaches' Pasta" seemed as good a name as any she could dream up. She could no longer give herself a reason for saying no. He would be gone soon, but she wanted to be with him until then. She knew he'd never make good on his threat, but would leave the final decision to her. As domineering as he sounded, he had always been protective of her. Why should she spend her nights alone when they could give each other comfort? When she could snuggle near his warm body?

She glanced at his anxious face. "Put that way, I accept. We'll tell them in the city. This is their weekend."

He breathed a huge sigh of relief. "What differences does it make when we tell them?"

"As far as they know, we haven't seen each other

during the week. If they think you offered me a job this fast, it'll sound suspicious. After the weekend sounds better."

"All right. As a matter of fact, Peaches' Pasta is a great name. I like the sound of it."

"It does have a nice ring to it," she agreed, calming down as he did. "As we've already said, if there are fast-food restaurants that specialize in stuffed potatoes, why not pasta?"

Jim suddenly stopped the car. Hungrily, he drew her into his arms. He kissed her long and lingeringly. When he released her, they talked more, fleshing out the idea that had begun when he had taken her to breakfast on Monday. More than financial profit, it afforded him a practical excuse for keeping his independent-minded lover at his side. He would let her run the pasta business.

"Is there a place for Dennis in your business?" she asked. "He's an excellent accountant. And he's put up with so much from me."

"All that Shakespeare." Jim grinned. "I'm grateful you kept him occupied in so cultural a manner. My people will run a check on him. If he's as good as you and he say, I'm sure we can use him in some capacity."

"Jim, you must understand my involvement is limited to your stay here and later what we accomplish by phone. I have obligations I can't turn my back on."

The heavy scent of pine permeated the car. He smiled in supposed agreement. He refused to argue and break the mood, and kept his emerging plans to himself.

Charlie sat on the dock, posing for Gerry. He glanced up often at her from the sketch pad propped

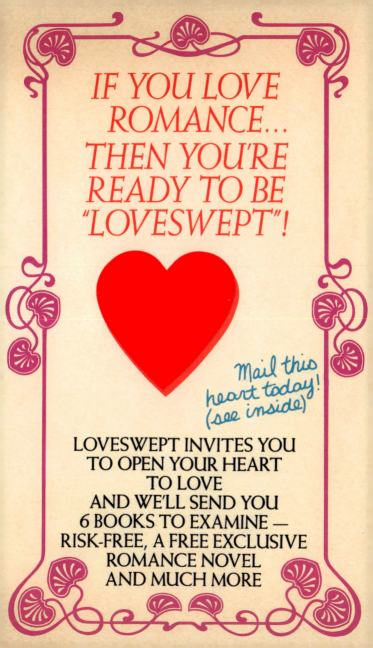

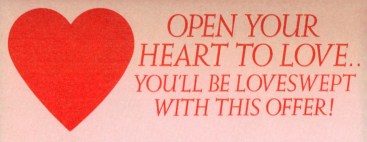

OPEN YOUR HEART TO LOVE..
YOU'LL BE LOVESWEPT WITH THIS OFFER!

HERE'S WHAT YOU GET:

1. **RISK-FREE! SIX NEW LOVESWEPT NOVELS!** Preview 6 beautiful stories filled with passion, romance, laughter and tears . . . exciting romances to stir the excitement of falling in love . . . again and again.

2. **FREE! AN EXCLUSIVE ROMANCE NOVEL!** You'll receive *Larger Than Life* by the best-selling author Kay Hooper ABSOLUTELY FREE. You won't find it in bookstores anywhere. Instead, it's reserved for you as our way of saying "thank you."

3. **SAVE! MONEY-SAVING HOME DELIVERY!** Join the Loveswept at-home reader service and we'll send you 6 new novels each month. You always get 15 days to preview them before you decide whether to keep it. Each book is yours for only $2.25 — a savings of 54¢ per book.

4. **BEAT THE CROWDS!** You'll always receive your Loveswept books before they are available in bookstores. You'll be the first to thrill to these exciting new stories.

BE LOVESWEPT TODAY — JUST COMPLETE, DETACH AND MAIL YOUR RISK-FREE ORDER CARD.

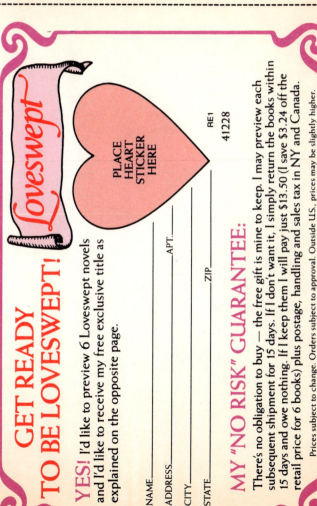

REMEMBER!

- The free gift is mine to keep!
- There is no obligation!
- I may preview each shipment for 15 days!
- I may cancel anytime!

(DETACH AND MAIL CARD TODAY.)

BUSINESS REPLY MAIL

FIRST CLASS MAIL   PERMIT NO. 2456   HICKSVILLE, NY

POSTAGE WILL BE PAID BY ADDRESSEE

LOVESWEPT
BANTAM DOUBLEDAY DELL DIRECT
PO BOX 985
HICKSVILLE   NY   11802-9827

NO POSTAGE
NECESSARY
IF MAILED
IN THE
UNITED STATES

on his lap. Her charcoal likeness was nearly completed.

"I can't wait to retire," he said. "Just think, we can go wherever we want."

"Surely you don't mean to travel constantly?" she asked, picking up the threads of an earlier conversation, one they'd left hanging. "What happens when the novelty wears off?" The minute she asked the question she realized she was putting him on the defensive. "Sorry, Gerry."

"Don't move your head. I get your meaning. I haven't given my retirement a whole lot of thought on purpose."

She gave him what she hoped was a look of understanding, but inside she fretted. "Gerry, I have people who depend on me, and I love what I do."

He added shading beneath her cheek to highlight her bone structure. "Why don't we drop the subject for now?"

"If we do, it will fester."

His jaw hardened. He added another charcoal stroke to the hairline. "Only if we let it."

He tore off the paper and handed it to her. He had drawn her exact likeness, yet he'd softened the edges, adding a touch of vulnerability around her mouth and a dreaminess to her eyes. "Gerry, this is very good. You're a real talent."

"I sketched a beautiful woman. Now hand me back my picture. I'm going to have it framed."

"I want one of you."

He leaned forward, bracing his arms on his legs. "You could have the real thing. Every night. In faroff places. We could see the sun rise in Japan, Australia, Europe. Take the Orient Express."

With a pang she knew she couldn't give him the answer he wanted, not if it meant turning her back on her work, or drastically altering her life-style to accommodate his. What he proposed sounded wonderful. As a vacation.

She focused on the nub of their problem: Marriage. Married people were supposed to be together as much as possible. But if she and Gerry had such different goals at the moment, then . . . "Gerry, I have the perfect solution." She smiled artlessly. "Let's *not* get married."

"What? Are you crazy?" The dock rocked as he stood up and stomped its length.

"Calm down and listen. Nothing will change." Her voice jangled nervously. "I wish you'd understand. I want you to be happy."

He shot her a look of pure disgust. "Stuff it, sweetheart!"

"Gerry, I'm taking the guilt away. You can retire, do the things you've dreamed of doing before we met, then, when you're home, we can be together. I'm offering you a man's dream. A warm bed with no responsibilities."

"You want to be my mistress, is that it?"

She recoiled. "I don't like that word."

"How about paramour?"

"Nor that," she said, stung by his imperious attitude.

"Then I suspect you wouldn't like sweetie, girlfriend, or main squeeze either?"

"You're right, I wouldn't!"

"Seeing as how you're being so all-powerful generous, how about passing me a few of the letters you receive, then? You want me to have a man's dream, I'll tell you a man's dream. I'll make some of your lonely readers the happiest women on earth. Better yet, you can tell them yourself that I take care of my woman. Print it in your column."

"Gerry, stop it!"

He glowered at her. "No way. You started this. You're the brain. I'm the dumb jerk who thought we had something important, something more precious than work and vacations. Shows you what I know. You're right. I do deserve the best of all possible worlds. I want a redhead here at the lake. You can be my city blonde—when you're not too busy working. The other times you can provide a substitute blonde. I'll take a brunette on my trips. Now, there's a man's dream. What could be better?"

Tears pooled in her eyes. She wiped them away. How had they gotten from laughing to this in the space of a minute?

"Perhaps I should go," she said, standing up.

His lips thinned. "What do I tell the kids? Or don't they matter?"

She'd forgotten about them. She didn't need Mary-beth feeling sorry for her, or for his son to give her the silent treatment for hurting his father. "All right. I'll stay until morning."

He nodded, then turned on his heel and strode up to the house.

Charlie stayed on the dock, staring out into space. Her chest hurt. She could barely swallow, her throat was so clogged with tears. Despite the warm sun, she felt cold. Her picture lay at her feet like unwanted litter. A sudden gust of wind blew it off the dock and into the water. She made a grab for it, but it was too far for her reach. She raced from the dock, her only thought to retrieve the picture.

Gerry stood on the porch, his hands jammed into his pockets, his spine ramrod stiff as he watched her. She halted, her feet frozen in place by his stony silence. He no longer cared. She spun around, sadly accepting the end of their relationship. At the railing she kept a teary-eyed vigil on the drawing. It slammed onto a rock near the shore. There it seemed to wait, as if giving them a last chance to change their minds, to salvage it, and to mend their future. From the porch came the creaking of a wicker rocker, the steady slapping of wood upon wood. The current loosened the drawing from its temporary mooring and careened it over the spillway.

Out of sight.

A great sadness welled within Charlie. Her past came back to mock her. She could still hear her husband's accusation. "It's all your fault. I never wanted to be saddled with a kid at my age. You tricked me. You put us in this predicament. You live with it."

He couldn't even acknowledge their baby was a girl. He called Marybeth an it. She stuffed her hand to her mouth to muffle her sobs as tears streamed down her face.

Eight

Jim offered to take everyone to dinner. He had worked up an appetite and wanted to eat. Charlie and Gerry declined, telling them to go, but Marybeth had been eying the huckleberry bushes and had a better idea.

She insisted on fixing one of her pasta and chicken specialties, with huckleberries for dessert. After preparing the ingredients for the main course, she asked Jim to light the barbecue grill, then went outside to pick huckleberries.

She headed for the bushes that grew on a hill a little way from the house, delighted to be cooking for more than two. When she was younger, she had longed for large family dinners with good conversation flying back and forth. It was one of the many things she had missed, growing up without a father. While four didn't qualify as a large number, it was a good start. She was starved, too, her appetite fueled by the afternoon's rigorous activities. She worked studiously, trimming the heavy branches laden down by the succulent fruit. She also ate half of the ripe, plump berries.

Jim watched her from the kitchen window. His heart swelled with love. Whatever Marybeth did, she did it with natural abandon. Gusto. When her tongue darted out to lick a trickle of juice from her mouth, he chuckled. Gerry, who'd walked into the kitchen for a soda, glanced out the window too.

"Looks like she's enjoying herself."

"Don't count on eating many berries tonight," Jim replied as his dad left the kitchen.

Suddenly Marybeth screamed. She jumped backward, dropping the berries. Without hesitation Jim sped out of the house, the screen door banging behind him. He reached her in seconds. Ashen-faced, shaken, she leapt into his arms. Trembling uncontrollably, she pasted herself to him, clinging as if for dear life.

"What's wrong?" he cried, her wide-eyed fright communicating itself to him.

Teeth chattering, she could hardly speak. "There's a . . ."

He cupped her face. "A what? Tell me."

Terrified, she gulped.

"Tell me."

She bobbed her head, her eyes wild. "Ssss . . . sn . . . snake." She blew the word on a great breath of air.

"You saw a snake?"

She clutched his neck. "T-tw-twelve feet. A boa constrictor!" Without looking in its direction, she pointed over his shoulder.

He choked back a laugh as well as a sigh of relief. The harmless garter snake, no more than eight inches long, slithered out of sight beneath a rock.

"It's gone, darling."

Still afraid, she buried her face in his neck. Applying gentle pressure, he tipped up her chin. "It's gone, I promise."

Mistrusting him, she stared at his sneakered feet. "Are you sure?" she mumbled.

He made her look at him again and see he was telling the truth. "Positive."

She peeked. All she saw was shrubs, grass, huckleberry bushes. Not even a bird or a squirrel. Like a prisoner set free from a hideous monster, she rewarded him. Her mouth on his, she blessed her savior.

Jim wasn't above taking credit for something he hadn't done, particularly when it led to such a fabulous reward. Only too glad to oblige, he kissed her back, preferring a dessert of her to huckleberries any day.

"Sweetheart," he said, coming up for air. She kept covering his face with gratitude. "Do you trust me?"

"With my life."

Perhaps he shouldn't tell her, just let her be grateful for the rest of her life. He shrugged off the sneaky thought. "The snake wasn't a boa."

She inched back. "A python?"

He smiled and affectionately tugged her hair. "I doubt it."

She pondered the information for a second. "A water moccasin?"

He rubbed her back. "Sorry, sweetheart. We're on land. Water moccasins don't walk."

She saw the sexy glint in his eye. "Then what kind of snake was it?" she demanded.

He tried to keep a straight face and lost. "More like a baby's shoelace."

"A baby's shoelace!" She huffed. With the danger over, she grew aware of how she must look and sound. "The trouble with you, James, is that you have no fear. It's disgusting. Abnormal."

He chuckled. "Peaches, my precious, five years ago you put fear into me. That"—he indicated the spot where the garter snake had disappeared—"is nothing. However, since you believe I saved you from certain death, now's a good time to ask."

"Ask me what?" She glanced nervously at where she'd seen the snake, as if to make certain it hadn't come out from its hiding place.

He cupped her face in his hands and looked directly into her eyes. "Peaches, you should marry me. You never know when you'll see another snake."

Thinking he was still teasing her, she kissed him again. "If you were in trouble, I'd save you."

He held her by the upper arms to create some space between them. "I'm serious. Will you marry me?"

The breath whooshed out of her. Marriage! James was asking her to marry him. She was being offered a loving place by his side. How could she deny her heart? She loved him. She'd never stopped loving him. Even if it meant an unusually long engagement until she cleared her debts, she'd figure out ways for them to be together. "Darling, of course I'll marry you!"

He grinned hugely, silently blessing the snake. Crushing her to him, he kissed her again and again. "Let's tell the folks."

She caressed his face, pressed her fingers to his lips. "James, I won't come to you with a dowry of debts. Please, it won't be long."

He pulled her hand down, his expression instantly changed. For several long moments he stared at her, needing time to convince himself to take heart from the fact that at least this time she'd agreed to marry him.

Her tremulous smile moderated his frustration. "You'll see," she said, laying a hand on his arm. "Everything will work out."

"When? Do you know how long it takes to accumulate the kind of money you need?"

Marybeth was reluctant to admit it could take a long time. James wasn't the most patient man in the world, she knew that. Furthermore, she knew other women would accept his financial help. Yet, she couldn't. She wanted to come to him, perhaps not as a full partner financially, but not as a burden. That meant living by her principles. Her mother had worked through adversity to attain success. She would earn hers too.

"You're set on this, aren't you?" he asked grimly. "You've got this idiotic notion that you need a clean balance sheet."

She dropped her hand from his arm. His face remained set.

"You make it sound so cut and dried," she said.

"Isn't it?"

"I can't help it. It's my belief system. Don't ask me to go into a long explanation. I'll be proud to be your wife. Let's first march our parents down the aisle, though. Darling, do this for me. Please keep this to ourselves for a little while. If we don't, we're liable to put undue pressure on our folks."

"Why?" he asked bluntly, but he might as well have been arguing with a brick wall. "My father's in love with your mother. He wants to marry her."

She spoke quickly, from the heart. "I'm sure my mother loves your father too. We're not taking anything away from our feelings for each other. After all, we never intended telling them we were in love just yet."

By the greatest effort at self-control, he tamped down the urge to kidnap her and find a justice of the peace to marry them immediately and work out the rest later.

She knew how to extract a promise from him, so he demanded one of his own. "I don't understand this obsession of yours, but I love you, so here's my final proposition. Peaches, this is the last time I'm asking you to marry me. You're no kid who needs time to grow up. I'm a man who wants a family. With you. You go ahead and sell your inventory, but tonight we tell the folks you've decided to help me with my pasta business."

Marybeth knew that if she refused, she'd lose him. "All right."

He gave her one last warning. "As long as you know I have no intention of letting you go or waiting forever."

She melted against him, thrilled they had come to an understanding. "Who else would save me from a shoelace? A child-size one at that?"

He tightened his arms around her. "Infant-size shoelaces. Like the babies we're going to make. You do want children don't you?" he asked gruffly.

When he gazed at her with that apprehensive look on his face, her heart melted. "As long as they're yours."

"Quick, Charlie, come in here!" Gerry called. He waved frantically in the air.

Alarmed at the urgency in his tone, she dashed into the kitchen. He grabbed her hand, tugging her over to the sink, then pointed out the open window. "When did that start?"

"Ohmigod!" Afraid her voice carried, she clamped her hand over her mouth. Eyes wide with shock, she stared in disbelief. Not fifty feet from them in front of the huckleberry bushes stood Jim and Marybeth locked in a kiss! Not an ordinary, friendly-type kiss, but a glued-from-head-to-toe kiss. From the way Jim cupped her daughter's buttocks, he was making sure even a sheet of onion skin couldn't get between them. For her part, her daughter had her arms wrapped around Jim's neck as if her life depended on it.

Eventually Jim ended the kiss. Through the open window Charlie and Gerry caught snatches of conversation.

Gerry thought first. "Come away from the window. When Jim went outside I was in the living room. I came in here to throw out the empty soda can."

Charlie nodded. Marybeth's interests were paramount. A wrong reaction was the last thing her daughter needed from her. It was she who had urged her to fall in love! In the bedroom, where she hurried with Gerry for a private discussion, she imagined her face mirrored the shock she saw on his.

He closed the door, then leaned an elbow on the dresser. She sat down on a chair. "Did you know?" he asked.

"Of course not! She never said a word."

"Jim didn't either."

Charlie wrung her hands. Alone with Gerry, acutely aware of the electricity between them, she forced herself to focus on their grown children.

"I should have guessed," she said, trying to quell her nervous tension. "I assumed they were friendly for our benefit. Marybeth knows my feelings about the need for families to get along." Gerry snorted, and she retaliated swiftly. "Acting ugly won't help in this situation."

He paced the length of the room. Several seconds passed. "You're right," he said. "I'm sorry. I acted childishly. The thing that gets me is that I'm a cop, trained to pick up clues."

"You're not on duty with your own son, Gerry, any more than I was with Marybeth." She repressed the desire to put her arms around him and seek comfort.

"I'm getting rusty," he muttered harshly. "Now that I think about it, there were signs. For instance, how did Marybeth know that Jim cuts his orange juice with extra water? Half the times she calls him James, when she catches herself she calls him Jim."

Charlie nodded. "And don't forget he reminded her to drink her orange juice this morning."

"She said, 'It's too early, don't you remember?'"

"You're right. And last night at cards, he knew she cheated. She accused him of having a memory like an elephant's. They didn't realize they were dropping clues. You heard him call her Peaches. I'm willing to bet they named the cat after my daughter."

"It's a sorrowful state of affairs when neither feels they could tell us about the other. We're a couple of dopes."

Charlie's fists clenched and unclenched. "That night when we came home and found them in the kitchen, they were totally relaxed. Like a couple who knows each other's habits."

"You heard Jim say they go back five years. Maybe more."

Charlie's back went up. Her eyes narrowed. "He's the man who broke my daughter's heart."

Gerry rallied to his son's defense. "Don't be so fast to place blame on Jim. Your daughter broke his heart too. I know for a fact he wanted to marry her. She refused."

That drew a surprised reaction. "He told you?"

"Not in so many words. I never knew the girl's name."

"You still don't," Charlie said lamely. "We could be jumping to conclusions. All we have are suspicions."

He scoffed at her reasoning. "From what we saw and heard, do you honestly believe that those two weren't in love before?"

"No," she admitted.

He grunted. "Sounds to me the daughter and the mother are greatly alike."

She rallied immediately. "Whether you or I approve, our kids are involved with each other. I for one don't intend to interfere. If I do, I'll push her right back into his arms."

"Meaning?" he demanded, his eyes impaling hers.

She crossed her arms over her chest. "It should be obvious. I hope it runs its course."

"Why? Because of me?"

She heard the fatigue behind the censure in his voice. He looked tired, his deep-set eyes marked by weariness. For them to have slept in the bed not a foot away from her, a bed they'd turned into a celebration of love and discovery, now seemed a dream. They were fast becoming strangers.

Gerry stared down at her. "We've come to a pretty pass, you and I."

"Impasse, Gerry. When that happens, it's best to cut your losses."

"Is that what Henrietta would say?"

She felt as if he were looking into her soul. "She just did."

He ran a hand through his hair. "As you say, they're adults. They'll tell us when they're ready."

"I'm glad you agree, since it settles one problem."

He threw her a sharp look. "There's more?"

"Us. We need to put on a good front. I'm no actress. After dinner I'm going to plead a headache. That will give me an excuse to be quiet."

Charlie was as good as her word. With no acting on her part, she complained of a headache at dinner.

The table was set with a centerpiece of wild roses. Marybeth had prepared a pasta with diced green peppers, black olives, and halved cherry tomatoes, as well as baked potatoes and green beans. Jim had grilled chicken breasts sautéed with lemon herbs. Charlie picked at her portion, letting the conversation go over her head.

"Mom?"

She blinked. "I'm sorry, Marybeth." She lifted her gaze from her hands, settling it on her animated daughter. "What were you saying?"

"Jim's offered me a job."

Jim chimed in. "Marybeth gave me the idea to open a pasta restaurant or add a pasta bar to our menu. A lot depends on location, feasibility, and testing the product. We're going to test her recipes."

Marybeth was beaming. "I like the idea of choosing from several dishes and sauces."

Jim nodded. "She'll tour some of my locations with me. We consider it on-the-job training. It should please you both."

"Why should it please me?" Charlie asked him point-blank.

Jim smiled, but his eyes were serious. "Unless I'm wrong, we're here this weekend to see if and how well we can get along. Marybeth's explained about the letters you receive from adults who don't approve when one of their divorced parents remarries. We know how you and my dad feel about each other, right, Marybeth?"

She smiled. "Yes, we want you to be happy. Gerry, you're a nice man. You're good for my mother. At first I was worried."

"Why is that?" he asked, his voice flat.

"It happened so fast."

Charlie put down her fork. Marybeth had uprooted her own words and flung them back at her. Falling for Gerry, initially pursuing him in her rush for happiness, she had overlooked a basic tenet for a good marriage. Marriage involved making a common emotional investment, a deal for life. Anything less ended in unhappinesses and divorce.

She looked from Jim to Marybeth. Five years ago they'd broken up; now they'd rediscovered each other. Obviously they couldn't wait to be together. At this point they'd say anything if they thought it would please her. It was written on their faces. She hadn't seen Marybeth this happy in years. She glowed. Her eyes shone. For Jim. As his did for her daughter. She just hoped he wouldn't hurt her again. The happy-family charade couldn't come at a worse time.

Gerry was watching Charlie. When she met his gaze a flicker of emotion crossed his face. "This calls for a toast." He filled her wineglass. "You do the honors, Charlie. You're better with words than I am."

She lifted her glass. "To you both. To you, Marybeth, and to you, Jim. I hope this proves to be all you want it to be."

They all drank, then Gerry raised his glass a second time. "Here's to financial success. And everlasting love." He swigged down his wine as if it were beer.

Jim raised his glass again. "To the success of

Peaches' Pasta and the inspiration behind it." He gazed warmly at Marybeth.

Charlie had had enough. Pleading the need for fresh air, she stepped outside on the porch. She ran her fingers through her hair, massaging her scalp. Closing her eyes, she slowly rolled her head from side to side, trying to relieve the crick in her neck. Behind her the door opened.

Gerry came outside and perched on the railing near her. "Are you all right?"

The light drained from her eyes, and her lips quivered. "I'm fine. I'd like to get an early start in the morning. There's usually a big pile of mail on Mondays."

"That's no problem," he said curtly, convincing her he was having no trouble distancing himself from her. "Do you read all the letters?"

"Yes. I consider that sacred."

"Charlie," he said in a low voice, "about the kids. What's this going to do to them?"

She shrugged. "By 'this,' I take it you mean us? Nothing." She was unable to hide her quavering tone that vibrated from hurt. "They'll accept the fact we changed our minds. There's no reason we can't remain friendly in their presence. It's not the first time this sort of thing has happened. After next week, you'll be off doing whatever you want to anyway."

His expression darkened. "Jim's asked to take us out after the retirement ceremony Thursday night. What do you want to do?"

"Go, I suppose. If I don't, they'll wonder why. We can let this die a natural death while you're away on a trip."

He stilled, then after a moment said, "You still got it all figured out, haven't you?"

"Gerry, we're marching to a different tune." She continued gazing out over the lake, not trusting herself to look at him. "Marybeth won't be shocked when I tell her we've changed our minds. She knows how important my career is to me. I've seen what happens to women who can't provide for themselves. Many end up taking emotional scraps, losing their sense of self-worth. Marybeth feels as I do about standing on her own two feet. That's the main reason she insists on shouldering her financial obligations alone, trying every avenue by herself first."

She chanced a look at him. His expression gave the impression she'd reached a wrong conclusion to a very serious subject. His words proved it.

"Has it ever occurred to you that you could be carrying this too far?"

Her irritation flared anew. "What makes it right for you to hold to your beliefs and not me?"

He slapped his thigh. "You're right. As for the sleeping arrangements tonight, I'll take the floor. There are extra pillows and blankets in the closet."

He straightened to his full commanding height. She was forced to look up at him, to let her gaze sweep past his chest and up to his rugged face. "Don't be silly," she said. "The space between the bed and the window isn't wide enough for a man your size to turn over. I'll sleep in the chair."

"Suit yourself. Good night, Charlie."

Her headache worse, she escaped to the bedroom. Closing the door behind her, she opened the dresser drawer and the closet. She packed her few things, ready for an early morning departure. She showered, put on her shortie nightgown, and wrapped herself in a blanket on the chair.

She couldn't wait to get back to work.

Pitch darkness cloaked Marybeth's bedroom. In a deep sleep she tried to turn over and couldn't. It didn't matter. She was in the midst of a wonderful dream. In it she observed two lovers in an idyllic secluded garden. Surrounded by majestic trees and summer air redolent with the scent of flowers, she wasn't frightened by the unaccustomed weight. She instinctively burrowed closer, welcoming its soothing security.

Toward dawn a sliver of light peeped through the window, shining into her eyes. Sighing, she rolled onto her side. Warm breath fanned her face. A muscled arm slung possessively over her hip, snagging her to its owner.

Her eyelids fluttered open. "What are you doing here?" she whispered to James.

He kissed her lips. "Would you believe sleepwalking?"

"No." She chuckled and playfully pushed him off.

"Mmm. I think I like mornings best."

"James?"

"Shhhh. Go to sleep."

"You're naked."

"So are you."

With a shock she came fully awake. She was buck naked and felt marvelous. "Did we do it?"

A low rumble erupted in his chest. "Would you believe me if I said we didn't?"

Her fingers tangled in his unruly hair. "How could I sleep through it? That's impossible, isn't it?"

He ran his hand over her breasts. She reacted instantly, making a faint sound of pleasure in the back of her throat. "I admit you hurt my feelings."

She snuggled next to him, feeding on his warmth. Her nose was cold, her body warm, the way she liked it. He clasped her to his chest, his hand roaming over her back. "Don't tell me you can't keep up with me, even in your sleep?"

She lifted the sheet covering their lower bodies. "James, at the risk of insulting you . . ." She giggled.

He recoiled in pretended affront. "You're a wench, an insatiable wench. I love you. I've never had a better vacation in my entire life."

She cocked her head. "Not restful, though?"

"No. Very uplifting."

"James, stop teasing. How long have you been here?"

He buried his face in her silken mane. "Mmmm, you taste better than your pasta. I'm going to print up a private menu."

She poked his shoulder. "Answer the question."

He sucked her nipple and she moaned, reaching for his head to hold him at her breast. Her heart was pounding, her breathing quick and shallow when he finally raised his head to look at her. "Tastes much better than pasta. How do you feel?"

She inhaled his musky scent. He looked boyishly mischievous and very satisfied. "Answer my question first."

"Sleepwalkers can't answer questions. It's part of our condition."

She gave up. "How long have you had your convenient problem?"

He grinned. "Who knows? The only thing I'm sure of is that you alone possess the medicine to ease my incurable condition."

She wrapped her arms around him and gave him a long kiss. "I love you, you crazy nut."

"I love you too. What am I supposed to do with this?"

He was hard, pressing into her. He rolled to the side, bringing her hand down to him. She gave him a gentle squeeze.

"Darling, this is a figment of your vivid imagination. None of this is happening. It's a dream. You're sleepwalking, remember?" She wasn't, though, and if she didn't get him into his own room soon, she'd prove it.

He grunted. "It's going to be hard for me to sleepwalk from Chicago. Change your mind. Come with me when I return."

She laughed. "You better sleepwalk back to your room."

His mouth took hers in a hungry kiss. "Party pooper."

"I'm no party pooper." Sitting up in bed with her hair tousled, the covers down around her waist, she gave him an engaging grin. "You're in the wrong dream. In my dream we did it."

In the bedroom on the other side of the house, Charlie awoke in the bed, not in the chair she'd discarded as uncomfortable, or the makeshift mattress of blankets she'd tossed on the floor. She had no idea how long she'd slept in the bed. She could only surmise that Gerry had lifted her from the drafty floor and tucked her in.

She was alone.

Nine

When Marybeth and Charlie arrived home on Monday, Marybeth found a message on her answering machine from Diana. She called her friend and got the good news that Diana had sold a bowl and a vase. She drove directly over there to replace the merchandise. They sat the new bowl and vase in a display case, then went into Diana's office. Diana took two sodas from her small refrigerator, handing one to Marybeth.

Sipping it, Marybeth used the calculator on Diana's desk to figure her recent earnings. Twirling a pencil between her fingers, she announced her good news.

"I've reduced my debt load by another five hundred dollars, not including the lamp bases I sold over the phone and my previous sales." She took a long drink. "If the man buys the bases, that'll knock off another three hundred."

Diana did her own quick figuring. "Let's see. You earned one thousand dollars in six months. That leaves nine thousand dollars. Say you sell two thousand dollars worth a year. With your brilliant thinking, you and Jim will glide down the aisle in four and a half years. Provided you have a groom."

Marybeth tossed her head. "He understands, even if you don't. You're playing with numbers. Anyone can do that."

Diana frowned. "Too bad you don't have my philosophy."

"Which is?"

"What's mine is mine, and what's yours is also mine. Seriously, friend, you're playing with fire. You and your mom are quite a pair. She didn't tell you she was dating Gerry until she was on the verge of marrying him. You haven't told her about Jim. When you do, you'll announce you are marrying him. In four and a half years. All in the name of independence."

A shadow crossed Marybeth's face. She yearned for a loving home with James by her side. Her father had shunted his family aside as unwanted baggage. He'd left a young wife, who had managed to translate adversity into success. But it had taken years, with many late nights spent honing her writing skills. Marybeth had observed the transformation and learned the importance of self-reliance—even as she has wished for a father.

Like her mother, though, she was made of sterner stuff. She brightened, saying confidently, "I'll work harder, prove your timetable wrong."

Diana rolled her eyes. "There's one good thing. If you do have to wait, you'll both still have your own teeth."

Marybeth swatted her.

Without using a calculator Jim knew he couldn't wait for Marybeth to sell her inventory in dribs and drabs. He needed a flawless plan to get her to the altar.

Abandoning all thoughts of waiting for his dad to marry Charlie first, he devised a strategy subject to modification. This being the most important goal in his life, and knowing Marybeth could carry her notion of independence too far, he choreographed his moves with precision.

Before he'd left her house after they'd returned from the country that morning, she'd given him all of her pasta recipes to fax to Chicago. Thanking her for each one became a mutual pleasure, since his idea of a proper thank-you had her willingly in his arms. She was a perfect flower, a ray of sunshine, a breath of welcome air. He didn't intend to have his lifeline cut off.

In his hotel room Jim checked and doubled-checked his list. Drawing a line through the first two items, he phoned his secretary. She updated him on the sales figures of a restaurant he'd opened in Dallas several months earlier, then he got to the main reason for his call.

"Nora, I need a credit and background check on Dennis Jorden." He supplied the necessary information. "Call me as soon as you get it."

Next, he called interior designers who specialized in restaurant decor. One said she was committed for the next two years to her supplier. The second, however, agreed to look at samples. If they were good, she would buy a few pieces. She herself loved the warm brown glazes, but she affirmed Marybeth's analysis, saying, "We sell the browns, but it takes longer."

Nora called back to report that Dennis Jorden enjoyed an excellent reputation. A graduate of the Wharton School of Business, he held a master's in economics and was highly respected in his field of forensic accounting.

Jim placed his last call to him. They set up a luncheon appointment at an Italian eatery overlooking the Hudson River. Traffic congestion made Jim ten minutes late. As he entered the restaurant, he spotted Dennis seated on the terrace beneath a wisteria-covered lattice roof. As he made his way toward the rear along a pathway lined with colorful impatiens, he ignored the bold, admiring female glances following him.

Shaking Dennis's hand, he slipped into the chair opposite him, thanking him for coming on short notice.

Dennis closed his menu. "I was curious. You're looking well. I trust you've been enjoying yourself with my ex-girlfriend."

Jim smiled. "We're getting married."

Dennis sighed. "Well, you have my blessings. I should tell you my heart's on the mend. I met a woman."

"That was quick. I hope you'll be very happy. What's her name?"

"Angel," Dennis said glumly.

Intrigued, Jim said, "You don't sound happy. How did you meet her?"

"She was sent to me."

Jim wondered if by *sent* Dennis referred to the world's oldest profession. "Come again?"

They interrupted their discussion as the waiter poured water into their glasses and set a basket of rolls and bread sticks on the table. After looking at the menu, each decided on ravioli.

"She's a jumper," Dennis said as the waiter left.

"You met her at a horse show?"

"Not exactly." He peeled the cellophane wrapper

from a bread stick. "The crazy kid jumps out of airplanes. She's a skydiver. She landed at my feet. I hope it's a good omen. You never can tell about these things."

Jim was starting to think he'd made a serious mistake about Dennis, who was sounding like a happy-go-lucky flake. Still, Marybeth liked him. And he hadn't earned his reputation by joking.

"I attended an air show," Dennis continued. "I strolled away from the cordoned-off area to the end of a deserted farm to be by myself. I've been licking my wounds. Thanks to you."

"You miss reading Shakespeare aloud?"

Dennis laughed. "Not on your life. I saw a chutist in trouble, blown away from the landing site, struggling for control. Naturally I ran with arms outstretched to save her. You can imagine my surprise."

"I can imagine hers. She must have been grateful for your help."

Dennis snorted. "Just the opposite. She yelled at me to get the hell away. Here I was, hopping around like a fireman holding a net. She was jerking the parachute strings, kicking her legs, and screaming at me that if I so much as put a hole in her chute she'd sue me for ruining expensive equipment. I stepped aside and dropped my arms. When she landed she whipped off her goggles and glared at me. I took one look at her and said destiny had brought us together."

Jim's lips twitched. "What did she say?"

"I memorized her words for posterity. 'Buster, I missed the mark. Destiny's got nothing to do with my misfortune of being blown off course. Wind sheer does.'

"I'd take up skydiving but I'm morbidly afraid of heights. Over five stories I get a nosebleed. She's a fiery redheaded angel. I'm going to marry her and we'll make beautiful babies. Little sun-blessed infants. *Who will never skydive.*"

Jim was laughing too much to eat his salad. "You're crazy."

Dennis's mouth curved downward. "Misery does that to me. It's been a tough week. Jilted twice. I assumed I'm here because you want me to audit your books?"

"They've been audited. I need a favor."

Dennis frowned. "What sort of favor?"

"I want you to help me clear Marybeth out of debt."

Dennis eyes him suspiciously. "Why me? You're rich. Write her a check."

"I tried. She refused it."

Their main course arrived, and both men dug into their food.

"The woman's got character," Dennis said. "So what's the favor?"

"It's about my contest. Legally, I can't enter it. Neither can a member of my family or anyone who works for me. Marybeth has agreed to help me expand into serving pasta at my restaurants, and has given me her recipes. Since she's not on the payroll yet, there's nothing to prevent you from entering one of her recipes. Here's my address. You don't need a form."

Dennis waved his fork at him. "Thanks but no thanks. I'll have nothing to do with doctored books or rigged contests."

His response didn't faze Jim. "I'll hire you as my accountant for the pasta chain."

"Or with bribery."

Jim tempered his ready retort. "While I appreciate your sterling character, this is on the up and up. I've checked you out, and besides, Marybeth asked me to find a place for you in the company."

Dennis leaned his elbows on the table. "An astute woman. Tell me more."

"The announced Quick Stop contest remains as explained in the ads and flyers. A completely different company is handling it. They will legitimately choose the winner. This is a side contest for one entrant. You mail it to me, I'll take care of the rest."

Dennis looked doubtful. "How will you make her believe a contest is announced one day and the winner is picked a few days later? This could backfire."

"Leave that to me," Jim said. He was still working out the details in his mind.

"I'll do it provided you do a favor for me. Your dad's a cop. I want to know everything I can about my angel."

"What's her name?"

"Roxanne Harris, which I learned later. After I was escorted from the air show by a security guard the size of King Kong." He sighed. "At least she didn't press charges for harassment, though for a minute there I thought she would."

Jim shook his head in bafflement. "Suppose your skydiver's married?"

"She's not." Fascinated, Jim asked him how he knew. "I just know," Dennis said with conviction.

Jim thought about Marybeth, how his body craved hers. For him it was real hunger, involving more than the physical act. In the years following their breakup, he hadn't been able to assuage the steady ache of being apart from her. In a manner of speaking, she was partly responsible for his success. He'd driven himself to prove he could live without her. What he had actually proved while his bank account mounted was that lasting success required loving. Marybeth and he were soulmates. Life without her, especially now that she'd let him back into her heart, would be unthinkable.

"Consider it done," Jim said. "If you're that observant, you must be a good forensic accountant. You see before you a man desperate to get married. I live in Chicago. I want Marybeth with me. I haven't the time or the inclination to wait. Do you know the names of the magazines where she sent her portfolio? She's heard from one. I want the others."

"Sure. I mailed them for her. Return receipt requested. I take it you plan on speeding up the process."

Jim nodded.

When he left the restaurant half an hour later, Jim had the information he needed. Back at his hotel suite he made a series of phone calls.

After returning from Diana's, Marybeth kept busy with a renewed sense of urgency. She tested a new pasta recipe and worked in the garage for several hours, filling a few orders. She applied for a booth at a flea market, then telephoned wholesale distributors in neighboring states, offering them an incentive of an extra ten percent discount on her selling price. One agreed to see her portfolio. He cautioned her that the public was high on cobalt blue and Southwestern Indian, but left the door open.

She was just cleaning up in the garage when the phone rang. She dashed in to the kitchen to breathlessly say hello.

"If you're panting," James said, chuckling, "I hope it's for me, darling."

"How did you know I needed to speak with you, to hear your voice, right this very second?"

"I love you. You send me messages, don't you know that? What do you want most in the world right now?" he asked, his voice a husky murmur.

She closed her eyes. To be free of debts, so that she wouldn't feel as if she were a failure who needed rescuing. "I want to be with you."

"That's my girl. We'll go out to dinner, then I want you to help me choose new uniforms. And Marybeth, it's time you told your mother about us. Even if you don't, you're still spending the night with me. I don't want to wait until we have to go out of town. I mean it, Marybeth. No more shadows. Our love is beautiful. We're going public."

Although she'd said they should wait for their parents to come to a decision about marrying, Marybeth knew James was right. They had loved each other for almost six years. That was longer than some people's marriages. And while they waited to marry, she could still show him her love. As he said, openly, with no sense of shame.

She found her mother in her spacious bedroom. Charlie's flair for color showed in the tasteful pastel's of soft greens and rose she'd used to accent the Georgian Court furniture. Framed photographs of Marybeth adorned the dresser.

Marybeth leaned against the doorjamb, watching her mother smooth a white cotton dress over her hips, then sit down at the vanity table. She began brushing her hair. Mother and daughter followed identical rituals. One hundred strokes, fifty forward, fifty backward.

As twilight fell, darkening the room, Marybeth turned on a lamp. "Where are you and Gerry headed tonight?" she asked when the brush strokes allowed her to see her mother's face.

"He's busy with last-minute things before he retires. I'm dining with Gladys tonight. She says she has something to discuss with me." Frowning, she added, "I've never had my secretary asked me out for dinner before. I bet it's bad news." She shrugged fatalistically, then asked, "What are you doing?"

"Jim wants my opinion on new uniforms he's considering. I never realized changing styles could cost millions of dollars."

Charlie caught her daughter's eyes. "You like him a lot, don't you?"

Grateful for her mother's question, she replied, "Yes. Do you mind? I mean with you and Gerry?"

Charlie didn't pause. "Darling, your happiness means more to me than anything in the world. Jim's a fine man."

Marybeth breathed easier. "He is, isn't he? Mom," she said earnestly. "We knew each other well when I was in college."

Charlie let the hairbrush rest in her lap. "How well?"

"We were in love. He wanted me to marry him, but I refused. I was too young." Marybeth had expected a surprised reaction from her mother, but she didn't get it.

"Are you in love with him now?" Charlie asked.

"I've never stopped. I love him now more than ever. He wants me to marry him."

Charlie pressed her fingers to her temples. "I see. Well, this is news, isn't it. And do you want to marry him?"

"Yes, as soon as I pay off my debts. He offered to pay them, but I refused. Have you and Gerry made any decisions about the future?"

"No, there's no rush."

"Isn't he planning a trip?"

Her gaze skittered away from Marybeth's. "He said he is."

Marybeth detected a change in her mother's voice. The ties between them were stronger than for many mothers and daughters. Her mother had never been able to hide her feelings from her.

"Mom, where do you fit into his life? I assumed you'd marry. Is there anything you want to discuss with me?"

"Never assume, darling. To answer your question, everything's fine between us. We understand each other completely."

Marybeth sat, then peered closely at her mother. Her eyes looked tired and her lips were pinched, as if she were in pain. Purple shadows smudged the area beneath her eyes. For once her mother's skin didn't glow. She had a sudden chilling thought.

"Mom, is your headache gone?"

She smiled wanly. "Not entirely. I had a busy day. Mondays are hectic."

"You should learn to use a computer instead of writing your columns out in longhand to give to Gladys. It would make your life easier."

"I know. Gladys says I should learn. I can't stand those monsters, though. I remember when I was in England, I had to hire a secretary to transcribe my notes for the book. I ended up making so many corrections, I might as well have not paid the price."

"That's why they have cut and paste, Mother. Don't stay out late tonight. You look pooped. What are you wearing to Gerry's retirement ceremony?"

"I haven't given it much thought. Now, scoot. I'll be late for dinner. Go."

Marybeth's heart fluttered with fear. Gerry's retirement was in a few days. The mother she knew would have tried on everything in her closet. For Gerry, she would even have purchased a new outfit.

Still thinking of the change in her mother, Marybeth showered and dressed. An hour later she melted into James's arms as she greeted him at her door.

His eyes twinkled. "I take it you can't stand to be apart from me?"

She wet her lips. "Shut up and kiss me."

"That's good enough." He locked her in a fierce embrace. She slid her hands inside her sport jacket to wrap her arms around him. She pressed her body to his at the same time he ground his closer.

"James," she said when he finally released her, "I told my mom about us. I'm relieved she knows."

He took her hand, keeping her close by his side, as they strolled to his car. "Me too. How did she react?"

Marybeth frowned with concern. "Briefly. It surprised me. She accepted it without asking a lot of questions. Other than saying she wants my happiness and that you're a fine man, she let it go at that. Don't you think it odd?"

"Your mom is a bright woman. It's not as if you're a child. To ask for details is digging up the past. She knows that. She's being considerate. Darling, you're wringing your hands for nothing. First you worried at the thought of telling her about us. Now you worry because she took it so well. We've passed the biggest hurdle. I know my dad. He'll be delighted."

When they arrived at his hotel, Jim let the valet park the car. Inside his suite, he fixed them both a drink, then led Marybeth to the sofa to sit down.

"I don't know," she said, still thinking about her

mother. "Mom's unusually quiet. I hope nothing's wrong."

"You're imagining things. My dad's as crazy about your mom as she is about him."

There was a silence then Marybeth said gently, "Jim, we felt that way too. We broke up."

"Isn't love enough?" he asked earnestly. "Shouldn't it be enough for us?"

He'd said that five years earlier. She caressed his cheek. He was remarkably handsome, she thought, even better-looking now than he had been before.

"We saw what happens when communication breaks down," she said. "We didn't communicate the way I feel we do now."

"Your father did a number on Charlie, didn't he?"

"Yes, but she was there when I needed her. She drummed the need to be independent into my head."

He put his hands tenderly on her face. "I'm here for you, Peaches. I'm not your dad. Can't you look at your debts as *our* obligation so we can get on with our lives?"

As before, she was grateful for his offer, but she still declined. He sighed. "Let's forget about it for now," she said. "Show me the uniform samples."

While she poured over the pictures, Jim considered all she'd said. He admired her mettle, her spunk, her willingness to clear her obligations. But he disagreed with her. Money, as far as he was concerned, should be shared with loved ones. The time to spend it was when someone needed help, not when everything was going well.

Marybeth chose a peach and burgundy polo shirt with burgundy pleated slacks. "Peach," she said, grinning, "is my favorite color."

"Come here," he said. He set the album of photographs aside and gazed at her with bold desire. "Do you realize it's been a whole day and my hunger has nothing to do with uniforms or other people?"

"You made dinner reservations."

His eyes hooded. He ran his lips softly across hers, then lowered his head. Cupping her breast in his hand, he pressed a heated kiss on the nipple, eliciting her instant moan of acquiescence.

"The hell with dinner reservations," he muttered, his hand slipping beneath her short chiffon skirt. "This hunger is more important." She nodded and they rose. He placed a warm hand on her back, leading her to the bedroom.

In the shadowed room they undressed slowly, taking their time to savor the freedom of being with each other. "You have the most exquisite body," he said, caressing her first with his eyes, then with his hands and mouth.

"I love you," she whispered, her arms around him, drawing him closer to her heart and body that throbbed for him.

"Always remember that I love you more. That anything I do, I do for us."

"I know," she murmured.

He fervently prayed, as he demonstrated his love that she would never have cause to regret her words. . . .

Ten

Charlie regretfully accepted the surprise resignation of her secretary, Gladys. Over their dinner, Gladys tearfully announced she was moving to Seattle.

"It's either that or lose my husband. He simply can't turn down this job transfer. I'll stay until you hire another secretary."

Sad to lose her, Charlie promised her a generous severance payment. Over the years they had built up a good rapport. They trusted each other. As she drove home, she mused that everyone she depended on was about to leave her. When Marybeth married Jim she'd move to Chicago. Gerry would be out of her life after the retirement party. Now Gladys, her right arm, would be clear across the continent.

With her mind dwelling on Marybeth's confession about her relationship with Jim, she swallowed her pride and phoned Gerry as soon as she got home.

"We were right," she said. "Marybeth and Jim are in love."

"I know. Jim called me a little while ago and said they're getting married."

"How do you feel about it?" she asked.

There was a long silence, then he sighed. "I'm not sure. It's awkward, to say the least."

Another long silence, then another deep sigh, this time from Charlie. "Gerry, we agreed to say nothing."

After a moment's hesitation, he asked where she was calling from. She said home.

"I'm coming over."

"There's nothing to discuss," she said despondently. She wasn't ready to see him. "It's out of my hands, and yours too."

He grew irritated. "You sound like hell. Why should it be the end of the world because our kids love each other?"

"It's not," she snapped. "It's just a mess." She shooed the cat away from the phone cord. "I wish Marybeth luck. She may need it."

"By that," he said, "I take it you're referring to me as his father?"

"Gerry, please stop this. Jim's hurt my daughter before. If he hurts her again, I'll throttle him."

"I don't get you. You just finished saying they're in love. How is he going to hurt her?"

"Love didn't help us. Good night, Gerry. My head's splitting."

"Have you eaten?" he demanded before she could hang up.

"Didn't you hear me?" she wailed. "I'm showering, then going to bed." She shook her head at the receiver as she heard him bark his question again. "Food's the last thing I want."

"When's the last time you ate?" he persisted.

Lethargic and miserable, she searched her mind. She hadn't been able to choke down any food at dinner after Gladys made her announcement. And

she didn't recall eating anything for lunch or breakfast. "Yesterday at the country," she said at last.

"No wonder. You're a bullheaded fool, Charlie.
First you make the honorable gesture of sleeping in
a chair. When that didn't work, you nobly go on the
drafty floor. There's no limit to your stubbornness."

"So it was you who put me to bed?"

"Who else would I let touch you?" he lashed out.
"You know you need a good eight hours sleep or you
get cranky. You're probably wired on caffeine right
now. Take your shower and get into bed. I'll be right
there."

"You will not."

"Don't argue with me, dammit! We wouldn't be in
this rotten fix if it weren't for your fancy ideas. Keep
your front door locked. I know how to get in."

"You do?" she asked, so astounded that she didn't
argue when he blamed her for being in what he
called this "rotten fix." As if their tattered romance
were all her fault!

"I can pick locks with the best of them. I learned
from a safecracker we sent up for twenty years." He
slammed the phone down before she could yell at
him to stay home.

Dispiritedly she knew it wouldn't help anyway.
Gerry always did what he pleased. On that miserable
conclusion, she left the porch light burning for him.

She showered, dousing her head under the warm
jets, hoping to erase her headache. Trailing puddles
on the bathroom floor, she swiped at the mirror over
the sink to clear the steam.

"Ugh!" she muttered. "I am a sad, pathetic-looking
specimen." She dissected her looks. Her mouth was
too full, her nose too small. Faint lines spread away
from her eyes and the corners of her mouth. She
stretched her neck and thought it wasn't too bad.

Yet. Next, she examined the backs of her hands. She wasn't ready for permanent gloves.

Still, she was well into her forties. "You're getting old, Charline. Love turned you into an old hag."

Then she did something she warned other women never to do. She set a hand mirror flat on the counter, then looked down at her face. "Ohmigod!" she yelped. "Gravity's got me."

She heard the front door open and close. Gerry shouted out he'd arrived, not to worry. By then she was crying.

He hurried up the stairs and knocked on the bathroom door. "I'm here," he said, announcing the obvious one more time.

"Go away." She sat on a stool, dripping wet and naked, her towel slung over her shoulder.

Gerry stepped cautiously into the room. Seeing her slumped on the stool, he grew alarmed.

"What's the matter?" he asked, crouching in front of her.

"Go away," she wailed.

"Not until you tell me what's wrong!"

"Can't you see? I'm getting old. Ancient. I'm an old hag. Go away."

He heaved a sigh of relief, trying his best to keep a straight face. "You're not old. And if you were, so what?"

"So what?" she asked tearfully. "It's easy for you to say. You're a man. Men get distinguished. Women age."

Unaware of his fascination with both her nudity and her logic, he asked, "Were you planning on letting the air dry you?"

"It's not right for you to see me undressed."

He closed the lid on the toilet and sat. "Why not?

I've tasted every inch of you, why shouldn't I see you naked?" He boldly let his gaze rove over her.

"That was yesterday. Or the day before. This is today. I bet you can't tell me the name of one female news anchor over the age of forty-five." When he couldn't, she smirked. "They pasteurized Jane Pauley."

"They what?" Gerry's shoulders shook.

"Took her off the *Today* program and put her out to pasture. Networks want young, beautiful girls, preferably blonde. I myself gave up girdles at forty."

"I consider that a blessing."

She glared at him. "We both know why, *Speedy*."

He grinned. "You're a caution, Charlie, my girl. Would you feel better if I strip and show you my old body? We can compare flab." His hands were at his belt.

"Very funny. You don't have flab," she muttered, knowing that if he were naked too, the bathroom mirrors would fog up even more.

"Neither do you." Without asking, he unceremoniously hoisted her off the stool. Lifting her chin with one finger, he gazed into her eyes. "Bloodshot. I swear, Charlie, you can't get along by yourself. You need police protection."

"Hah. I saw where that got me. Except for aging overnight, I'm fine."

"Sure you are, honey."

Aside from the fact that her knees felt as if they were buckling, aside from the fact that in her naked state she wanted to melt in Gerry's arms, aside from the fact that she had to force her own arms to stay stiffly by her sides, aside from the low fire stoking in the pit of her belly, she was fine.

"Lift your arms," he commanded.

"No."

"Never mind." He raised them for her, wrapping the towel under her armpits and securing it around her body. Then he patted her with his big hands, paying particular attention to her breasts, thighs, and buttocks.

The man was a demon, Charlie decided. He could work magic through a towel. He was wearing stone-washed jeans. Gerry, in jeans, bulged in the right places. Gerry devastated her senses. She didn't know what game he was up to now. He had been so furious with her, he'd let her picture drown. Now he was being achingly sweet.

She hated him.

She gulped sadly. She had drowned as surely as her picture had. As angry as he had been then, he was as gentle with her now. It was all very confusing.

He sat her on the stool, found another towel, and began to dry her hair. He fluffed it with his fingers, then kneaded her scalp. Spotting the hair dryer on the counter, he switched it on to medium heat. She sat like a rag doll, letting him style her hair with mousse. When he finished, he massaged her neck and shoulders. Moving in circular motions, his thumbs soothed the tight cords on her neck, at the base of her skull, behind her ears.

"Do you like that?" he asked as his talented fingers worked their way over her scalp.

She went limp, offering no protest. When he gently tilted her head to the side, she let her cheek rest on one of his hands.

He laughed. "I take it you do." He switched on the hair dryer again, playing with her hair. Her eyelids drooped.

"Mmm," she purred. How could she lie? Gerry had all the right moves. "It's heavenly."

"You poor little darling."

"Old darling," she muttered, yawning. "I lost my secretary today. Gladys is leaving. Marybeth is leaving. Everyone's leaving. You included."

"Right." He eased her up again. "You're all tuckered out from the trouble you caused me."

"Gerry," she mumbled.

He held her upper arms and gazed lovingly at her sleepy face. "Yes, old darling?"

She scowled at him. "You're an idiot."

He chuckled deep in his throat. He peeled away the towel. "Would you like me to kiss you now?"

She yawned. "It won't change anything. I still hate what you did."

At least she hadn't said she hated him, he thought. He rubbed his lips sensuously across hers. "I know. One kiss can't hurt."

A tear slid down her cheek. "You drowned my picture."

"Please forgive me?"

"I don't think I can."

"Try. Please. I'm sorry. One kiss?"

"No."

"Think of it as payment for my drying your hair."

"No."

"Then think of it any way you want." He pulled her naked body to him and gave her a scorching kiss.

Somehow her hands slid around his neck. His raced over her, robbing her of all thought save one. If he were wearing his mirrored shades, she'd be in serious trouble right now.

Gerry didn't bother to count. One wasn't satisfactory. It demanded a second. The second expected a third. The third introduced the fourth, and so on. Fortunately, Charlie was too sleepy to count, so he thoroughly reacquainted himself with her mouth. Being without her, suffering the pain of their separation, however briefly, had driven him wild. If she hadn't phoned him, he would have phoned her. He'd rather fight with her than be alone.

Far from satisfied, he lay her gently down on the bed, then opened the dresser drawer where she kept her nightgowns. He rifled through them, shaking out the sexier ones for his inspection. Like Charlie's house, the drawer reflected its neat owner. Everything in place, uncluttered, orderly, tidy.

He had never dressed her before, only undressed her. He liked the idea of performing intimate tasks for her. He chose a lacy bit of black froth cut low in front and back. She allowed him to pull it over her head, then smooth it down with his hands. Her breasts grazed his chest. It nearly undid him.

He gathered her in his arms. "Charlie," he said with a groan, "this is very hard on me. Literally, darling."

She patted his chin. "Gerry, I'm going to miss you. Tomorrow I'll line up a brunette for you to take on your trip."

"Say it again and I'll dye your hair brown," he growled.

He sat with her long after she'd fallen asleep, a paper and pencil in his hand. Much later he rose, going downstairs to the kitchen. He put the chicken soup and roast beef sandwich he'd brought for her supper in the refrigerator. She needed rest even more than food.

There was still the matter of their children to discuss. Who knew where that would end? He didn't want Marybeth or Jim hurt. But they were adults, apparently with a long romantic history. They would work out their future. At the front door he paused, his gaze traveling up the stairs. His thoughts had been with her all day. More than anything, he wanted to be with Charlie, to fall asleep with her in his arms, be the first to greet her in the morning. One thing he swore to himself, and he said it aloud. "You're not going to miss me, Charlie. Regardless of what happens to our kids, I'm determined to work this out. Tonight proved it."

When the alarm rang the next morning, Charlie's eyes popped open. A note from Gerry sat on her nightstand. She hopped out of bed and raised the blinds, letting the early morning sun stream into the room, then read the note.

"You were too tired to make sense last night. I trust your headache is gone. We'll talk."

So much for hearts and flowers, she thought. No one could accuse Gerry of being a poet. Not only was her headache gone, she had a very clear memory of him blaming her for all their troubles. So much for her weak moment. . . .

The floor and chairs were littered with nightgowns he'd apparently rejected. No one could accuse him of being Mr. Neat, either. She glanced at herself in the mirror. "Ohmigod!" she screeched. Her hair stood in spikes around her head. She looked like the Statue of Liberty!

And no one could accuse him of being a hair stylist. She ran to the bathroom and turned on the shower.

Marybeth tiptoed upstairs to find her mother's bed made, her room as empty as the house. While waiting for the tub to fill, she checked her answering machine. Two hangups. Undressing quickly, she eased down into the tub. She let her mind fall backward to the incredibly passionate night she'd spent with James. He'd driven her nearly delirious with want, torturing her by suckling hard on her breasts while his fingers teased her warm, moist center. When she hadn't been able to stand a second more, she'd pulled him down on her with a strength she hadn't known she had.

Exhausted and replete, she had fallen into a deep sleep, only to be awakened by him as the gray fingers of dawn slipped through the partially drawn drapes. "Last night wasn't enough," he said huskily. "It's never going to be enough."

It was so tempting to give in, let him clear her debts and go with him to Chicago. For all of her life, though, she had admired her mother's courage. As her role model, her mother set the standard, the example that adults of both sexes should be able to care for themselves.

Her bath over, Marybeth donned shorts and a cotton blouse. A cup of tea in hand, her cobbler's apron in the other, she entered the garage. She had just finished applying a flow glaze to a pair of lamp bases when the phone rang early that afternoon. Expecting James, she found herself speaking to a Robert Connaught. He identified himself as an interior decorator.

"I saw the portfolio you sent to Armie Bouchard." He mentioned the name of one of the magazines she'd contacted, then added, "I'm leaving for England day after tomorrow. Would it be too much of an imposition if I drove out now to see your work?"

Thrilled yet managing to sound cool and business-like, she gave him directions to her house. He arrived an hour later. A diminutive man, he had eyes and hair the color of walnuts, as was his suit. She led him to the living room, where she'd displayed selections of her pottery. Butterflies fluttered in her stomach as he made his inspection.

"The pictures you sent Bouchard showed talent," Mr. Connaught said. "Seeing these pieces proves it. I'm buying for a collector who knows quality, and who prefers neutral colors rather than vivid ones that can clash with a decor. If it's all right with you, I'd like to send my truck for it in the morning."

"It?" she repeated.

She'd expected him to buy a few pieces. When he clarified that he could use the entire inventory, since he had other clients whom he knew would want them, she was stunned. It took all her self-control to contain her joy. After he'd handed her a check and left, she phoned Diana.

"About that timetable, Di." Learning her good news, Diana squealed. Later Marybeth realized that in her excitement she failed to learn the collector's name. On the way to the bank to deposit the check, she made a mental note to phone Robert Connaught.

It was a day filled with surprises. She'd no sooner returned home when Dennis phoned to say he had entered one of her recipes in the Quick Stop contest. He explained he'd been worried about her financial situation, and that he knew she would never enter the contest.

"I forgive you," she said. "But the odds are I won't win."

James picked her up at six and they drove to his hotel. Inside his suite, he checked for messages. His secretary had called. He called her back and quickly settled some minor problems.

Turning to Marybeth, he smiled. "How does it feel to have no worries?"

Arms extended, face flushed, and eyes bright, she whirled around the room, bumping the sofa and narrowly missing a wall. She sank onto a chair, flinging her arms out and kicking off her sandals, sending them flying in opposite directions.

"I love Robert Connaught!" she declared, and launched into a description of him, making him sound like every woman's heart's desire. Suave. Debonair. Sexy. An Adonis.

James frowned, and she grinned at him. "Okay, he's not as good-looking as you. I still adore him. He's got fabulous taste!"

"In other words, you feel good."

"Terrific. If I'm dreaming, I don't want to wake up. I feel as if a ten-ton load has been lifted from my shoulders. I feel as if the joy of Christmas has taken up permanent residence in my heart. I feel as if I've won the lottery."

She jumped up from the chair and bounced over to the window. She ran her fingers down the beige mini blinds, pinging the plastic blades against the glass. "I never imagined how good I would feel to give my mother her house back. Have you any idea how often we've stubbed our toes on those crates? And guess what?"

"What?"

She threw her arms around his neck. His hands slid down her spine, keeping her close. The glint of mischievous humor sparkled in her eyes. "Dennis, my ex-lover, phoned!"

He cheerfully shook her. "Your ex nothing!"

She smirked at him. "That sweet man worried about my finances. How could I be angry with him for entering me in your contest? We'll still have to wait to get married now. The terms clearly state no member of your family or employee is allowed to enter."

Glowering, Jim asked, "How do you know? Did he show you the entry form?"

"No, but I'm right, aren't I?"

Jim's own spirits plummeted. Obviously, the phony contest was not one of his better ideas. "This is insane. Tomorrow we'll go to City Hall and get the license."

She laid two fingers across his lips, silencing him. "Nope. Patience. Patience. A wife," she went on, suggestively nudging her hips against his, "is about as close a family member as you're going to get. At least this wife plans to be. Dennis said the winner is going to be chosen soon. How soon?"

Jim said in two weeks. He almost said the next day, but thought better of it. He silently cursed himself. Marybeth, on an adrenaline high, applauded Dennis for trying to help her, blessed Robert Connaught, and made him jealous of himself!

"You'll come to Chicago in the meantime?" he asked hopefully.

"No. I couldn't possibly. On the outside chance I'd win, how would it look if your staff sees us together? It's collusion."

He'd done an excellent job of skunking himself! "For goodness' sake! What do you care? They're going to see us together the rest of our lives! What's the difference? You'll be working with me in the pasta business."

"That and pottery." She gave him a loud, sucking kiss on the neck. "There! I've branded you. How many children do you want? I want a son. I want him to be exactly like you. In every way. He's going to have the best father in the world. Kind. Handsome. Loving. A good sense of humor. Honorable. Honest. Darling, I'm so happy."

Although he had no right to her glowing description of him, he knew that if it were in his power, he would gladly lay the world at her feet to see her this joyous. His body shuddered with an involuntary rush of need. Grabbing her, he plundered her mouth. He inhaled the delicate scent of her perfume. Alluring, bewitching, captivating . . . He could run through the entire alphabet describing her and still not do her beauty justice. Every other woman paled in comparison. He kissed her with a hunger fueled by the knowledge that she was the most important person in his life. He needed more than her silky, sensuous comfort, more than raw passion, more than a physical release.

"I love you, Peaches," he said, looking deeply into her eyes. "I have for years. Nothing would give me greater happiness than for us to marry. For us to start a family."

She broke into a wide smile. "The pleasure will be all mine. Well . . . not exactly."

He shook the silly imp's shoulders. "Not exactly?"

"Your body is hard, trim, male. And that's the way it's going to stay. Have you any idea how many women's heads turn when you enter a room?"

"At the very least, I've come to expect them to stand up and cheer," he said with sham solemnity. "What's my killer charm got to do with us getting pregnant?"

She looped her arms around his waist. "Us. What a lovely word. A shared experience. I don't relish morning sickness, backaches, swollen ankles, and frequent trips to the bathroom. Since we are going to be full and equal partners, you may have that part."

"Thank you," he said in mock appreciation. He felt his heart trip. The lamp cast a shimmering glow on her face, and her hair was a nimbus of golden highlights shot through a crown of lushly rich chest-nut.

Half an hour later Jim let out a reluctant sigh. Her mood was so playful and she was so exuberant, he gave up trying to seduce her. Making love to a frolicsome Marybeth in a mischievous mood was like trying to hold a slippery eel.

When she wound down, he tried again. This time very successfully . . .

Eleven

Marybeth wouldn't take no for an answer. "The stores at the mall are open late," she told her mother. "We'll both buy new dresses. It'll be girls' night out."

Charlie agreed rather than make a fuss. Her world was changing and she might as well accept the inevitable. Still, she hadn't been able to take Gerry's phone calls for the past two days. She didn't want to hear him blame her again for ending their love affair. She'd instructed Gladys to tell him she'd see him Thursday night when he picked her up for his retirement party.

Feeling anything but festive, she spent an hour choosing an appropriate gift for his retirement. Actually, she bought him two: an electronic multilanguage dictionary and a wristwatch with a continuous readout of the various time zones, so when he traveled he wouldn't need to set his watch for local time. She instructed the shop to send it to his home, but found writing the gift card a wrenching experience.

They tried four department stores for dresses with

no success. In the fifth store, a fashion boutique specializing in small sizes, the clerk brought out a white satin dinner suit with a pearl-embroidered bustier.

"You look positively scrumptious!" Marybeth declared when her mother tried it on.

Charlie wished she felt positively scrumptious. It was good to see her daughter's infectious happiness, though. She veritably bubbled with joy.

At Charlie's recommendation, Marybeth bought a deep purple silk-crepe dress. Tight and with a low V neck, it came only to mid-thigh.

"You're young," Charlie said. "You can carry it off." At the salesclerk's suggestion Marybeth also bought rhinestone earrings with crystal teardrops. They both purchased silk shoes; Charlie's in white, Marybeth's in black.

"Mom," Marybeth said as they headed home, "you still haven't told me your plans. Tomorrow night's Gerry's retirement. Has he said what he's going to do?"

In a steady voice that belied her inner turmoil, Charlie said, "As far as I know, he's making up his mind whether he wants to take a cruise or fly over to Europe."

"And then?" Marybeth prompted.

Charlie shrugged. "Then he'll decide. He's worked hard all his life. He wants a chance to do nothing and see what it's like."

"Mom, are things okay with you two?"

She nodded. "But I hate losing Gladys."

"You should learn how to use a computer. We're almost in the twenty-first century, you know."

"Now I really feel old. Do you use a computer?"

Marybeth grinned. "Nope."

• • •

While the women were shopping, Jim visited his dad. Gerry looked worried, not like a man about to retire without a care in the world.

"How's Charlie?" Jim asked.

"Fine. How's Marybeth?"

"Fine."

Gerry flipped channels on the television with the remote control switch. He sat, then he rose. He laughed shortly. "Don't mind me. That's the first time we've had such a short conversation."

Jim sat down. "Maybe it's time we had a long one."

Gerry nodded. "You're right. I'd like nothing better."

They spoke for several hours. Father and son loved mother and daughter, and neither could count on walking down the aisle anytime soon.

"I may have to kidnap Charlie."

"I've thought the same about Marybeth."

The mantel clock chimed ten times as both men sat with their long legs extended, their arms hanging over the sides of their chairs.

"I still don't know how to solve my problem with Charlie, I made a giant blooper."

"Suppose," Jim began slowly, and sketched out a possible solution.

"I like it," Gerry said, becoming greatly enthused. "It could work. Providing we both want it to. It could solve everything. I wish I had thought of it. Charlie didn't want you and Marybeth to know we've had a falling out."

"Marybeth is the original do-it-yourselfer. I know all about falling outs. I fell in love with her the day I met her. In all these years, I could never get her out of my mind. Believe me, I tried."

"I'm glad it's working out for you, son. But her mother, not Marybeth, is the original do-it-yourselfer."

Jim wandered over to the window. He leaned an elbow on the sill and gazed down at the tree-lined street. He wasn't home free yet. Thinking of his machinations with Marybeth, he remembered Dennis's request and relayed it to Gerry.

"Doesn't it seem odd he'd go to such lengths to learn about a woman who let him be taken to jail?" Gerry asked.

Jim refilled his glass. "No more strange than the pair of us."

Gerry gave Jim a dubious look. "We're in love. What's his excuse?"

"He thinks it's love at first sight."

Gerry grunted. "More power to him. If it is love at first sight, he's got my congratulations. Love at second sight takes some working out."

Jim walked back to his chair. "You're right. All you can do is try and hope you're doing the right thing."

The next night Jim was more convinced than ever that Marybeth was the prettiest woman in the world. The strength of his desire stunned him. Her green eyes glowing with tenderness, her glistening hair styled in loose waves about her shoulders, she descended the staircase.

"You're magnificent," he said, admiring the sexy yet elegant dress. Her long legs were encased in stockings with tiny jets that caught the light as she moved. He kissed her softly on the mouth, his tongue grazing her lips and sending a clear erotic message, a message he also naughtily whispered in her ear.

His suggestive, lopsided smile made Marybeth's

heart stop. In his white dinner jacket that fit his frame with tailored perfection, he looked fabulous.

"I'm going to hold you to that," she said.

Her words brought a broad smile to his lips. "Gerry's planned a surprise for your mom," he said mysteriously. "It's at my hotel suite. We'll stop by there after the party."

Charlie descended the stairs then. She had never seen Gerry in a tuxedo, and the sight of him, the raw strength of his body so elegantly clad, electrified her senses.

He seemed equally awestruck by her. "You look . . . incredibly young," he said. "Beautiful. I meant to say beautiful." He glanced at the fancy top. "This is for you." He held out a florist's box. On a bed of satin lay a delicate white orchid, its petals rimmed in pale lavender.

He shifted slightly. "I guess you don't want to wear this, what with those pearls and all." He shrugged. "What do you call that?"

"A bustier. I'm glad you like it."

"Every other man will like it too," he muttered.

Beginning to feel wonderful, she took the box from his hand. "Would you like me to wear it in my hair?"

He smiled, and she saw the flecks of gold reflected in his eyes. "I'll help."

"No thanks." She laughed. "I've seen your work."

The tension set aside. Charlie returned to her bedroom, and anchored the orchid in her hair with pearl-tipped hairpins. When she went back to the living room, Gerry gazed at her with approval.

The banquet room in the catering hall was filled with policemen and women and the top brass. They were all in the mood to have fun. Gerry introduced Charlie to so many people, she couldn't remember one name. A committee from his precinct had gathered a collection of anecdotes. Set to music, the occasionally raunchy lyrics were in good fun. Besides the good-natured ribbing, Gerry received many official commendations.

Jim and Marybeth beamed with pride. His hand strayed to the back of her neck. "Much as I'm happy to be here," he whispered, "I'm going to be a lot happier when we're home alone."

Gerry's farewell speech brought a lump to Jim's throat as his father told the audience of his pride in his son. He spoke of his work in the police force, and the friendships he had made in the department. He ended by looking squarely at Charlie. "Thank you for being by my side tonight."

As people applauded, no one but he and Charlie knew that might be the last time he would say that. Charlie dabbed her eyes.

They made their good-byes and left. Jim had ordered chilled champagne and chocolate-dipped strawberries for them in his hotel suite. Gerry's "surprise" was a misshapen grouping of objects hidden beneath a white sheet. A red bow lay on top.

"I'm getting out of this jacket and tie," Jim said. "Pop, you do the honors with the champagne."

"What can I do?" Charlie asked.

"Sit down and be beautiful," Gerry said. His color was high with excitement. Marybeth noticed the red message light blinking on the phone and told Jim.

"Get it for me please," he called as he walked into the bedroom. "I'll be right in."

She called the operator and asked for Mr. Davis's messages. There were three. The first was from Nora, the second was from one of his vice presidents. When she heard the third, she stiffened, then blanched.

"Would you repeat that, please?"

The operator did, and Marybeth shuddered. She

collapsed into herself like a drowning woman whose fingers couldn't quite reach the life saver. Her eyes swam with tears. Her throat clogged. How was she going to get through the next few hours?

In his shirt-sleeves, James came up behind her and kissed her neck. "You smell delicious. Nothing earth-shattering, I presume."

Unable to speak, she handed him the messages. He pocketed them without looking at them and threw an arm around her shoulders.

She drew in a sharp breath, catching his attention. "Are you okay, honey?" he asked.

"I'm fine," she said, her voice tight. "Let's not keep Gerry waiting."

"Something's wrong," he said flatly, carefully not to alert Gerry and Charlie. They sat on the other side of the room, quietly talking. "What is it?"

Marybeth stiffened. She lifted her head, letting him see the anguish in her eyes. "You should be very happy, James. All your plans have materialized."

"What are you talking about?" he asked.

Gerry broke in. "Come on, you two. Charlie's antsy for her presents."

Marybeth threw a bright look on her face and walked over to them. Jim stayed where he was, his eyebrows drawn together in a worried line. He gazed at her in bewilderment, mentally reviewing the evening. At dinner she had sat by his side, an enchanting partner in every way, gracious to one and all. The ride back to the hotel had been uneventful. So what had set her off? Whatever it was, it happened after they got to his suite.

His dad had uncorked the champagne. While he'd gone into his bedroom to remove his dinner jacket, Charlie had sat on the couch and Marybeth had called the desk for his phone messages.

The phone messages!

Digging into his pocket, he found the three slips of paper and read them quickly. Nothing. Nothing. Ohmigod!

His gaze flew to Marybeth. She met it fiercely. If looks could kill, he'd be dead. "Would you excuse us please?"

Gerry shook his head. "Not now. Whatever you want to say can wait. I want to give Charlie her presents."

Both Jim and Marybeth remained frozen in place while Gerry lifted his glass.

"A toast," he said. "A toast to the Wynston women. We love you. Right, Jim?" Without waiting, he went on. "I wish I could claim this as my idea, Charlie, but it's Jim's. He figured out how we can stay together."

A strangled cough had their gazes swiveling to Marybeth. Ashen-faced, her eyes swimming with tears, she swiftly dug in her purse for a tissue. "Sorry, Gerry," she mumbled. "Please go on."

Charlie jumped up. "Marybeth, why are you crying?"

"Crying?" Gerry repeated. "How can she be crying? This is a party."

Jim crossed the room and grabbed Marybeth's hand. "We'll be right out. Everything's fine, Dad. Show Charlie her gifts."

Marybeth flung his hand away and stood. "I'm not feeling very well. It must be the rich food I ate. Please, don't let me ruin your party. I'm sorry, Mom. Jim, you stay. I'll take a cab home."

"Stop being so damned sorry for yourself and sit down!" he thundered. "Since you refuse to do this in private, we'll do it in public."

"Jim, I'm warning you."

He held up his hands. "No. No more threats, no

more pussyfooting around you, no more anything, Marybeth. I've had all I can take. Folks, this couldn't come at a worse time. For that I'm sorry."

"What are you talking about?" Charlie asked.

"That goes for me too," Gerry said. "This is supposed to be a party. What in hell's gotten into you two?"

Jim pointed at Marybeth. "Your daughter, Charlie, has just discovered the horrible truth."

Charlie's eyes widened. "What horrible truth?"

He tossed the notes down on the table. "I'm Santa Claus."

"Oh, shut up!" Marybeth yelled. "What Jim is saying is that he paid my debts. This . . . this . . ."

"Overbearing clod," Jim supplied.

"Thank you. He is now the owner of all my pottery. This . . . this . . ."

"Underhanded scum."

"Underhanded scum!" She snorted. "Is none other than the secret collector who sent Robert Connaught. I fell for it. I actually thought I was doing this by myself. But he's my mysterious benefactor. Who needs the pottery like I need a hole in the head! Connaught left a message the shipment is on its way to Chicago."

Dumbfounded, Charlie and Gerry glanced at each other. "Is that why she's mad?" Gerry asked.

"Hush," Charlie said. "Jim's not through."

"Oh yes he is!" Marybeth said.

He glared at her. "No, I'm not. You might as well know the rest so you can feel twice as justified. I asked Dennis to enter you in a phony contest. What's more, he supplied the names of the art directors to me."

She gasped. "Dennis! I don't believe you. He's too honorable."

He nailed her with a look of pure disgust. "Right. And we all know I'm not! Call Dennis. You might wish him luck instead of giving him hell. He's found someone to love. Oh, there's one more thing. You were right. I don't need your pasta recipes. I wanted them only to get you. To give you something to call your own. But no more. Who can live with all these crazy restrictions? I bow to your self-sufficiency. You don't need anyone but yourself."

Her eyes sizzled. "Why did you do it?"

"He loves you," Gerry interjected.

Jim ran a hand through his hair, his expression as cold as the words he said.

"That's over. Dead. I'm through being a fool. I must have been out of my mind. You don't need me. You'd lock out any man who gets too close. I can't compare with the debts you wear like a hair shirt."

Marybeth smarted under his charge. "How can you say that? I prided myself on not being a burden to you. Why didn't you ask me?"

"I did," he replied wearily. "I offered to pay your debts outright. I offered to loan you money. I offered you a job. *I offered you me, dammit!* I offered us a home, a future. Nothing worked. You win."

He paced the room. "You talk about burdens. Well, life is full of burdens. You'll never be free of them. What's more, you don't want to be. The irony of this is that if I gave you a ten-carat diamond engagement ring, you'd take it. But a check, forget it! Charlie, you're a great mother and nice lady. But in your own way you're as wrong as Marybeth."

"How dare you?" Marybeth screeched.

"Now, see here!" Gerry exclaimed at the same time. "You can't talk to her that way."

Charlie's eyes were wide with disbelief. And curiosity. She was the only calm one in the room. "Let him speak. First, though, Jim, pour me another glass of champagne. Then I want everybody to sit down. After that, Jim, you may list my shortcomings."

Gerry snatched the wine bottle and refilled Charlie's glass. He threw an angry look at Jim. "Charlie, why don't we just go?"

She shook her head. "I want to hear what Jim has to say."

"Jim, I'm warning you—" Gerry added.

Charlie tugged Gerry's sleeve, then patted the sofa. When he sat, she tucked her hand through his arm, anchoring him.

"Now, young man," she began. "Marybeth, where do you think you're going?"

She had scooped up her purse and her hand was on the doorknob. "Home. I'll call a cab."

"Sit down." The order sliced through the air.

Marybeth sat.

Jim shot Charlie an admiring glance. "Okay," he said, slapping his hands together. "I admit five years ago Marybeth was too young to marry, and I shouldn't have pushed her."

"Thank you," Marybeth said sourly.

"I'm advising you to be quiet," he told her, then turned back to Charlie. "Marybeth's no baby. At least not in chronological terms. She's an infant when it comes to taking what's offered to her, with no strings attached. Maybe one day she'll learn that love, offered freely, generously, shouldn't be discarded, but should be nurtured. Cherished."

"Marriage has to be based on mutual respect and trust," Marybeth said. "With each partner full and equal."

Jim crossed over to her. His back to Charlie and Gerry, he spoke to her.

"You're right. But you were then and still are now afraid to fully trust. You're petrified of it. I'm not talking money here, Marybeth."

Her eyes on him, she asked, "What are you talking about?"

"Trust. Commitment. A core of security no one can take away. Real partnership. I'm not the father who abandoned you. You kept placing obstacles in my path. When I offered to buy the pottery, you said no. When I offered a loan, you said no. Yet you praised Dennis for entering you in my contest without your permission. You even wanted to delay our wedding to see if you'd win that contest. You thought Robert Connaught was the greatest man on earth for finding a collector to buy your work. You loved it when someone helped you out, as long as the person wasn't me. That was getting too close, too risky. Ask yourself why you accept from strangers and not from a man who loves you? Am I any less a man, less worthy than they?"

The tears spilled down Marybeth's cheeks.

"In the country," he went on, "you said you would help me if I were in trouble. But that has to go two ways, Marybeth."

"Excuse me, Jim," Charlie said. "You started to talk to me. Finish it."

Jim faced her. "You're a brave woman, Charlie. But you're too brave. Too independent. A man has to be able to give to the woman he loves. He hurts when he sees her in pain or struggling. There are all kinds of debts beside financial. Your husband did a cruel and stupid thing. Out of the failure of your marriage, you built a career. While you were doing that you also built a fence around yourself. The fence had room for one other person inside it. I think you know who I mean."

"Son." Gerry stood. "No, Charlie, don't stop me. He's not going to give my speech. I am. Charlie, I'm in love with you. What's more, you're in love with me. If these young pups need to work out their differences, they can do it on their time, not mine. I hope they're not stupid, but if they are, I'm not letting it interfere with our future. We're getting married. Period. I'm not asking, I'm telling. We're old enough, thank goodness, that I don't have to play the women's lib game. Don't get me wrong. I'm for equality in most things. But I'm a man and you're a woman. We have certain needs we satisfy in each other. Furthermore, you and I are going to have it all. You can go right on being Henrietta Heartfelt to your heart's content. I understand your need to work. You can spout all the advice you want. Where you do the spouting from is open for discussion, however. I'm taking care of you from now on, and you're taking care of me. It might not be a bed of roses, but there are going to be two people in the bed. You and me. Is that clear?"

Charlie thought the only thing missing was his mirrored sunshades. Everything else was perfect. The wide masculine stance. The strong hands jammed in his pockets. The rugged jaw. Even the bossy mouth that spouted a lot of words from sheer terror that she would refuse him.

"Yes, dear."

His knees nearly buckling, Gerry let out a huge breath of relief. Charlie threw her arms around his neck to give him a kiss so steamy, Marybeth and Jim averted their eyes.

When Gerry finally ended the kiss, he was grinning from ear to ear. "Good." He assumed the bossy nature Charlie adored. "Now, sweetheart, you come on over here and see your presents."

He escorted her to the table. "Go ahead. Remove the sheet, darling. Jim, would you mind taking Marybeth somewhere else? This is special. Private. Between a man and his future wife. I don't need you two spoiling our moment."

Marybeth's gaze locked with Jim's. He nodded stonily, and the two went into his bedroom. Needing to fix her face, she quickly fled into the adjoining bathroom.

"Go ahead," Gerry said to Charlie. "Take it off now."

She swept the sheet off with a flourish. There on the table sat enough electronic equipment to take her into the next century. "What is all this?" she blurted out.

"Freedom." At her dubious look, he chuckled. "Darling, it's not as bad as sucking a lemon. I forgot. You don't like gadgets much, do you?"

"No, I love them," she said unconvincingly, afraid to disappoint him.

Like a kid turned loose in his favorite hobby shop, he showed her the goodies. "Two computers, honey. One is a laptop. And here. Two laser printers. This tiny one we can take with us when we travel. And this here's a fax machine. I had them insert a fax board in the laptop. You'll be able to send your columns to the paper as quick as you can blink your eye."

She smiled weakly.

His hands shook as he placed a cardboard tube into hers. His voice went all soft. "This is for you, Charlie. With all my love. Go ahead. Open it."

She didn't have the heart to tell him she didn't know the first thing about computers or fax machines or laser printers and didn't want to learn. She supposed whatever was in the tube belonged with the array of wizardry on the table. She withdrew a rolled paper, and he hovered over her as she smoothed it out.

She gasped. With the utmost care she spread the paper on the table and gazed at it, scarcely believing her eyes.

"Oh, Gerry," she said, her voice choked. "I love you, you big lug. You rescued me. I didn't drown. You saved my picture. Jim was right. All these years I've been giving advice and hiding behind my own fears. That day in the country—" She started to cry.

"Hey." Gerry dabbed his own wet eyes, then gathered her close. "Are you going to do that every time I draw a picture of you? I went out that night with a flashlight and found it stuck on a rock. See, the charcoal didn't blur. Sweetheart, about what I said in the country. I didn't understand then. I know what it's like to be scared. I acted like a jerk. I love you. How could I go away and leave you? What kind of future is that?"

She swiped at her eyes. "I wasn't fair to Marybeth. I wanted her to be so strong, so independent. I ruined her life."

"Shh. She's got Jim. Don't mind what he said. He's not leaving her so fast. He's got too many years invested."

She sniffled. "You heard him. He's cutting her and Peaches Pasta out of his life. Marybeth loves him. I know she does."

"Darling, it's their lives. She's a fine woman. She's your daughter. My money's on my son. I didn't raise a fool."

She snuggled into his embrace. "Gerry, you're so wise. I need you so. Do you think you can help me with my column? Give me a man's point of view?"

He backed up, holding her at arm's length. "Just

as long as you understand I'm no Mr. Henrietta Heartfelt."

"Of course, dear."

He grinned. "With all the time I'm going to have, I'll type your columns onto the laptop when we're away. Or in the city when we're home. If you like, I'll teach you how to use this stuff."

She shook her head. "I'd rather have a live-in helper. We could work in the country. You can prepare your one-man art show there."

"My what?"

She picked up her picture. "Gerry, you're so talented. I'll pose for you, provided you do one thing for me." Pulling his head down, she whispered in his ear.

"Aw, do I have to?" he grumbled.

Firm on this, she nodded. "Gerry, I've said yes to everything you asked of me."

"In bed too?"

She grinned. "You know what those mirrored shades do to me."

He pulled her to him for a long kiss. "We're leaving. I've got a hankering to wear my sunglasses."

Twelve

Her mind numb, James's stunning denunciation still ringing in her ears, Marybeth stared at her reflection in the bathroom mirror. She tasted the bitter realization that in winning the battle, she'd lost her future.

Tense shoulder muscles made it difficult to hold up her head. He'd accused her of being afraid to risk. Of being fearful to cross the threshold to absolute trust. Was he right? If she couldn't face the truth, she'd go through life as an emotional cripple. His words echoed in her mind. Had she hidden behind terms like *independence* and *self-reliance*, using them as a shield against the fear of rejection if she were seen as less than perfect?

He had cited her praise of others who meant less to her. He'd charged her with fear of making the commitment that would allow him to be an integral part of her life. He'd defined burden as part of sharing, taking the sting out of the meaning of the word. Risking and accepting life's joys and burdens, joining hands to forge a stronger link. A family. By her attitude she'd fed his belief that she didn't need him. Nothing could be further from the truth. She had to show him she'd made a terrible mistake.

He knocked on the bathroom door. "They've gone. Let's go."

She stepped into the bedroom. He was a proud man. By trying to make certain he'd never have cause to leave her, she'd done the opposite.

"Have I really been so selfish, James?" she asked shakily, her voice filled with sorrow.

"Yes." Without another word he walked out of the bedroom into the living room. She was aware of his tension, as if he could no longer stand being in the same room with her.

"Get your purse," he said as she followed him. "I'll take you home."

She never dreamed it would come to this. She felt like a wounded animal, trapped and bleeding as life slipped away. She would never feel his gentle touch again, see his teasing smile.

She'd had five years of missing him. Now she would have a lifetime. Acting on blind instinct, she gathered herself and squared her shoulders. "I'm thirsty. May I have a drink first?"

She sat on the sofa and crossed her legs.

He said nothing. He poured the rest of the champagne for her and handed her the glass, then sat in a chair, drumming his fingers on the armrests.

"I ruined your dad's retirement party."

His exasperation evident, he shrugged.

She eyed all the electronic equipment and latched onto it to try to get him to talk.

"My mother doesn't know the first thing about computers. I suppose your dad will teach her. She's in love with him. She's too smart to let him go. She's not the fool I am."

Music played softly on the radio, a romantic ballad. He switched it off. He spoke then, his voice harsh and gruff. "Can we go? Postmortems bore me."

"I'm indebted to you," she said, desperate to get him to talk with her.

Jim slapped his thighs, cutting her off. "Do me a favor. You don't owe me any money. I'll chalk all this up to a lesson learned. Drink up and let's get the hell out of here. I've got work to do. Tomorrow I'm leaving. I'm going home, where I belong."

Trembling inside, her nerves stretched to breaking, she purposely nursed her drink. "When you were talking about fences before, you made me think."

"Marybeth, I am not in the mood for philosophical discussions."

She kicked off her shoes. It was a calculated risk, but she grabbed at it. "May I have a strawberry, please?"

He shoved the dish of chocolate-covered berries in her direction. She picked one up. She knew she would gag if she tried to eat it, so she simply held it.

Faced with his ironclad will, dismay and regret rippled through her. She couldn't fault her father. He was old news. She had never known him, yet only now did she comprehend that on a subconscious level she had held herself up to a standard that included fear of rejection. Yes, she still believed in being independent, but not when it meant shutting out the people who loved her. To give love she had to be able to accept it. Had the positions been reversed, she would have moved heaven and earth to help James. By every measure, he was the finest man she had ever met. She didn't know how to right the hurt she'd caused him.

Morosely, she began to absently tap her toe on the

carpet, tracing the green design. She stared down at her foot. At her toes. Suddenly she dropped the strawberry on the coffee table. She set her glass down, too, and rose.

"Excuse me. I'll be right out. Then you can take me home."

Inside his bedroom, she closed the door. Her chest hurt. She could barely swallow. Despite the warmth of the room, she felt cold. She flung open his clothes closet and crouched down. Working quickly, she got what she needed and placed them on his pillow. With her heart beating double time, she wrote a note on paper she found on the night table. She placed it atop the pillow, then walked back into the living room.

"I'm ready."

Without a word, he stood. Her body began to move effortlessly to his. She checked herself in time and gazed at his face, his dark, unreadable eyes. They walked in silence to the elevator. She felt sick to her stomach.

His bearing stiff, distant, he punched the down button, then he patted his suit pocket. "I forgot my car keys."

The elevator arrived before he returned. She stepped in, riding it alone to the lobby. There was no reason to extend the torture. At the front entrance, she asked the doorman to call her a cab.

"If Mr. Davis comes looking for me," she added, "will you tell him I've gone on ahead."

"It'll be a few minutes, miss."

She nodded, then stepped out into the night. The wind had kicked up, blowing her hair, teasing the hem of her short skirt. A man glanced appreciatively at her long legs and smiled. She didn't even notice. A cab pulled up, and the doorman opened the door for her. As she started to move toward it, a firm hand clasped her arm. James whirled her around.

Breathing hard, as if he'd run a marathon, he thrust her note in her face. In his other hand he clutched the items she had placed on his pillow.

"Did you mean it?" he asked.

She wet her lips. She tried to speak, but no words would come.

He shook her. "Do you mean this?"

"Yes. Yes. Yes. I need you, James. I love you."

"Cancel the cab," he said to the doorman. With her at his side, he hurried back to the elevator. It was waiting, and he hauled her inside.

"How did you know this was the one way you could make me listen?"

Her eyes were hopeful, her voice shakey. "I didn't. I prayed. You were there for me when I was in trouble. I thought if I put them on your pillow, you'd understand how sorry I am, how much I need you. I couldn't find the words to tell you I was afraid. I didn't know it myself. You were so cold."

"Say them now. I need to hear them."

She trembled. "I—I don't want to live without you. I don't want to live my life inside an emotional fence. I love you. I want us to be a family. I love you."

He cupped her face in his hands. Wild hope beat in her heart when she saw his gaze become tender.

"Peaches, no more tricks, no more fears. I respect you for wanting to be self-reliant, but when it hurts you, I need you to come to me just as I'd come to you. I love you. We're going to be a team in every way. You can be as independent as you want as long as you know I'm part of it."

She bobbed her head. "You've been part of me for so long, I wouldn't want to live without you. What you said about fences, about me keeping you out . . .

When I realized how I hurt you, and why I'd done it, I couldn't stand myself." She started crying. "James, if it makes you happy, I'll spend all of your money."

His lopsided grin sent her heart soaring. "Our money, but don't go overboard. We're going to have to start saving for our children's college education."

"James, I'm so sorry. I almost lost the best father my children could ever have."

He put his fingers to her lips. "Shh. No more."

He led her directly to the bedroom of his suite. "All right. First we need to do this. Tell me the names of these so you can show me how much you need me."

With loving attention to detail, she unfurled his fist and removed one brown shoelace. She grimaced theatrically. "This one's a water moccasin."

"Don't be frightened," he said, and gave a soft kiss. "Did that help?"

She nodded and pulled out a longer shoelace. A black one. She shuddered. "This one's a boa constrictor."

He kissed her harder this time. His tongue delved inside her mouth to mate with hers. Curing her of her fear of boa constrictors took a long time.

She eyed the next shoelace with horror. "Ugh! This one is a python. I'm terrified of pythons." She shivered deliciously as he dipped his head and through her dress covered one nipple with his mouth.

"Not python, James. Pythons!"

"Sorry. I forgot how demanding you can be." He gave loving attention to her other breast.

His hands unzipped her dress, then he backed her up to the bed, forcing her to sit. Kneeling down, he removed her stockings, his hands teasing her naked thighs. She took out another shoelace.

"This one is . . . Oh!" Her breathing became shallow and rapid.

"I know, darling," he murmured. "I hate bringing up business at a time like this, but I am an entrepreneur. Will you head up Peaches Pasta?"

With him kissing the juncture of her thighs, she moaned. "I'll do anything you want. I'll head up the whole empire, just don't stop! Oh, James!"

He set to work in earnest.

"I can't for the life of me remember the name of the snake you're curing me of now. Ohmigod."

He kissed her inner thigh. "A diamond-headed rattler. Would you mind getting in bed? I do my best protective work between the sheets."

She grabbed the remaining shoelaces, freeing his hands so he could strip. Naked and beautiful in her eyes, he gathered her in his arms. Her eyes glowed with love for him.

"Now, let's see," he said. "Where were we?"

Where they were had her gasping. Where they were had her tossing the shoelaces onto the floor. "James!" she exclaimed, arching her hips. "Do you think you can manage without the rest of the snakes?"

With the sheet over his head, and with him magically curing her fright, his "why" was muffled.

She cried out as he took her over the edge. "I want to save them for when you sleepwalk."

THE EDITOR'S CORNER

Next month LOVESWEPT brings you spirited heroines and to-die-for heroes in stories that explore romance in all its forms—sensuous, sweet, heartwarming, and funny. And the title of each novel is so deliciously compelling, you won't know which one to read first.

There's no better way to describe Gavin Magadan than as a **LEAN MEAN LOVING MACHINE**, LOVESWEPT #546, by Sandra Chastain, for in his boots and tight jeans he is one dangerously handsome hunk. And Stacy Lanham has made a bet to vamp him! How can she play the seducer when she's much better at replacing spark plugs than setting off sparks? Gavin shows her the way, though, when he lets himself be charmed by the lady whose lips he yearns to kiss. Sandra has created a winner with this enthralling story.

In **SLOW BURN,** LOVESWEPT #547, by Cindy Gerard, passion heats to a boiling point between Joanna Taylor and Adam Dursky. When he takes on the job of handyman in her lodge, she's drawn to a loneliness in him that echoes her own, and she longs for his strong embrace with a fierce desire. Can a redheaded rebel who's given up on love heal the pain of a tough renegade? The intensity of Cindy's writing makes this a richly emotional tale you'll long remember.

In Linda Jenkins's newest LOVESWEPT, #548, Sam Wonder *is* **MR. WONDERFUL,** a heart-stopping combination of muscles and cool sophistication. But he's furious when Trina Bartok shows up at his Ozarks resort, convinced she's just the latest candidate in his father's endless matchmaking. Still, he can't deny the sensual current that crackles between them, and when Trina makes it clear she's there only for a temporary job, he resolves to make her a permanent part of his life. Be sure not to miss this treat from Linda.

Judy Gill's offering for the month, **SUMMER LOVER**, LOVESWEPT #549, will have you thinking summer may be the most romantic season of all—although romance is the furthest thing from Donna Mailer's mind when she goes to Gray Kincaid's office to refuse his offer to buy her uncle's failing campground business. After all, the Kincaid family nearly ruined her life. But Gray's passionate persuasion soon has her sweetly surrendering amid tangled sheets. Judy's handling of this story is nothing less than superb.

Most LOVESWEPTs end with the hero and heroine happily deciding to marry, but Olivia Rupprecht, who has quickly developed a reputation for daring to be different, begins **I DO!**, #550, with Sol Standish in the Middle East and Mariah Garnett in the Midwest exchanging wedding vows through the telephone—and that's before they ever lay eyes on each other. When they finally come face-to-face, will their innocent love survive the test of harsh reality? Olivia will take your breath away with this original and stunning romance.

INTIMATE VIEW by Diane Pershing, LOVESWEPT #551, will send you flying in a whirlwind of exquisite sensation. Ben Kane certainly feels that way when he glimpses a goddess rising naked from the ocean. He resented being in a small California town to run a cable franchise until he sees Nell Pritchard and she fires his blood—enough to make him risk the danger of pursuing the solitary spitfire whose sanctuary he's invaded. Diane's second LOVE-SWEPT proves she's one of the finest newcomers to the genre.

On sale this month from FANFARE are three marvelous novels. The historical romance **HEATHER AND VELVET** showcases the exciting talent of a rising star—Teresa Medeiros. Her marvelous touch for creating memorable characters and her exquisite feel for portraying passion and emotion shine in this grand adventure of love between a bookish orphan and a notorious highwayman known as the Dreadful Scot Bandit. Ranging from the storm-swept English countryside to the wild moors of Scotland, **HEATHER AND VELVET** has garnered the following praise from *New York Times* bestselling author Amanda Quick: "A terrific tale full of larger-than-life characters and thrilling romance." Teresa Medeiros—a name to watch for.

Lush, dramatic, and poignant, **LADY HELLFIRE,** by Suzanne Robinson, is an immensely thrilling historical romance. Its hero, Alexis de Granville, Marquess of Richfield, is a cold-blooded rogue whose tragic—and possibly violent—past has hardened his heart to love . . . until he melts at the fiery touch of Kate Grey's sensual embrace.

Anna Eberhardt, whose short romances have been published under the pseudonym Tiffany White, has been nominated for *Romantic Times*'s Career Achievement award for Most Sensual Romance in a series. Now she delivers **WHISPERED HEAT,** a compelling contemporary novel of love lost, then regained. When Slader Reems is freed after five years of being wrongly imprisoned, he sets out to reclaim everything that was taken from him—including Lissa Jamison.

Also on sale this month, in the Doubleday hardcover edition, is **LIGHTNING,** by critically acclaimed Patricia Potter. During the Civil War, nobody was a better Confederate blockade runner than Englishman Adrian Cabot, but Lauren Bradley swore to stop him. Together they would be swept into passion's treacherous sea, tasting deeply of ecstasy and the danger of war.

Happy reading!

With warmest wishes,

Nita Taublib
Associate Publisher
LOVESWEPT and FANFARE

From the Bestselling Author of
THE MORGAN WOMEN
and **THE FLAMES OF VENGEANCE**

THE FIREBIRDS
by Beverly Byrne

*A glorious, sweeping novel of passionate intrigue, romantic mystery,
and a proud woman's passion for truth.*

They were bound by a centuries-old conspiracy of secrecy and
scandal . . . generations of the mighty Mendozas have conquered
persecution and treachery to become one of the world's most powerful families. Now one valiant woman seeks the truth of her
heritage . . . and threatens to destroy them all.

England 1939
Murder shatters the peace of the countryside, and a beautiful society
matron disappears without a trace. Few know that behind the shock-
ing crime stands the House of Mendoza . . . a secret the rulers of
the dynasty are sworn to protect.

London 1970
An indomitable young woman seeks to rip aside the curtain that
obscures her past. Armed only with her wits and her desperate need
to know, clever and courageous Lili Cramer pits herself against the
power of the Mendozas and finds terror, truth . . . and a love she
will never forget.

New York 1980
A man learns that he can close his mind to the sins of his family, but he
cannot erase the memory of the only woman who has ever touched his
heart.

From the hot and hectic streets of New York, to the cool and gracious
manors of the English aristocracy, to the sun-drenched palaces of

southern Spain . . . echoes of the past ignite a blaze in the present. Only the Firebirds can rise triumphant from the ashes.

Prologue

England: 1939

At a few minutes past two P.M. on the seventh of April, a single ray of sunlight glimmered on the sodden earth of a rainswept garden in Sussex. Lady Swanning tipped her extremely pretty young face upward and felt the welcome warmth. At that moment she heard the first cuckoo of spring.

The bird's distinctive call echoed in the stillness of the garden. It was Good Friday, and most of the staff of the great house had been released from their duties for the afternoon. Lady Swanning and the bird had the far-flung lawns and the beds of tender spring flowers entirely to themselves.

She thought about the cuckoo. Somewhere it would find the nest of another bird and deposit one of its eggs. When the hatchlings emerged, the cuckoo baby would destroy the rightful children, either by pecking them to death or pushing them to the ground. The conscripted foster parents, unaware of how they'd been duped, would nurture the changeling. Lady Swanning believed the cuckoo was a marvelously clever creature.

The sunlight faded and another bank of clouds rolled across the Sussex downs. Lady Swanning glanced at her elegant gold watch. Two-thirty, almost time. Casting a last look at the garden, she began walking toward the great stone house built centuries before.

How sad that she must leave all this. She had loved her life since marriage, adored the excitement of race meetings and dinner parties and balls, thrived on being the feted and admired young wife of Emery Preston-Wilde, the thirteenth Viscount Swanning.

Regret did not alter her decision.

As she had anticipated, the servants had left for church and the house was hushed and still. Lady Swanning and her husband were also expected to attend the service. Emery was to read one of the lessons, as his forebears had done for generations. This year would be different, for reasons which only Lady Swanning understood.

In the gun room she quickly found what she wanted, a Mauser that Emery had appropriated from a German officer in the Great War. Like all her husband's guns, the pistol was oiled and ready. To become a lethal weapon it had only to be loaded with the cartridges kept in a locked drawer in the sixteenth-century Jacobean cabinet. The night before, while Emery slept, she'd taken the key. It had been quite simple.

Loaded now, the small snub-nosed pistol fit easily into the pocket of her tweed jacket. Lady Swanning returned to the long corridor, her footsteps making no sound on the Oriental carpet. Moments later she stood before the study door and looked again at her watch. It was two forty-five.

"I'll be in my study," her husband had said at lunch. "Meet me there and we'll go on to church. Say, quarter to three?" He'd looked up from his poached salmon. "Do try for once to be on time, my dear."

She was exactly on time. Lady Swanning smiled, then went in. Emery stood with his back to her, staring out the tall French doors that led to a walled rose garden. He was a big man. His form blotted out much of the gray light. "Damned rain's starting again," he said without looking around.

"Yes." She took the pistol from her pocket and thumbed off the safety catch. It made only the tiniest sound.

"Well, nothing for it, we have to go."

"No," she said quietly. "I don't think so. Not today."

"Don't be silly. There's no way we can—" He turned, an expression of annoyance on his face. Then he saw the gun. "What are you doing with that?"

She didn't answer. It seemed to her unnecessary since her intention must be obvious.

The cook, the parlor maid, the chauffeur, and her ladyship's social secretary were the skeleton staff in the house that afternoon. At five minutes to three the cook and the maid heard two explosive noises and ran to the study. They found Lord Swanning lying facedown in a pool of blood. Their first impression was that he'd fallen and injured himself. The cook struggled to roll the viscount over. That's when she saw his staring eyes and the gaping, bloody wound in his chest and began to scream.

The chauffeur and the secretary arrived within moments, summoned by the screams, though both subsequently denied hearing the shots.

Lady Swanning was nowhere to be found. The police looked long and hard—until a few months later when war broke out and diverted them—but she seemed to have vanished from the earth.

FORTUNE'S CHILD
by Pamela Simpson

Twenty years ago, Christina Fortune disappeared. Now she's come home to claim what's rightfully hers. But is she an heiress . . . or an imposter?

She was a woman of ambitious dreams

Other women had claimed to be Christina Fortune, missing heiress to one of the world's largest shipping empires. Now this beautiful, self-assured woman had stepped out of the shadows of the past, daring to take what she insisted was hers.

She was a woman of mystery

Her heart was tormented by yesterday's secrets. What happened twenty years ago to drive a sheltered fifteen-year-old away from her privileged life, her wealthy family, and into the dark and dangerous city streets? Where had Christina gone? And what was she running from?

She was a woman of fortune

She had promises to keep—to the girl she once was, and to another. Now, from San Francisco to Hawaii to exotic Hong Kong, she must fight to gain control of the family business, fight to convince them all that she is Christina. But the hardest fight of all will be against her own blossoming desire . . . for a man she dares not trust, a man who has too much to lose if she is who she claims.

Christina looked around her at the lush coconut palm grove that dotted the crescent-shaped, white sand beach; the small, shallow lagoon; the massive stone wall formed from lava that once flowed here; and a tall, narrow, thatched building.

"*Pu'uhonua*," she whispered. Then, looking at Ross, she translated, "It means *place of refuge*."

"Do you remember it?" Ross asked, watching her carefully.

She knew perfectly well what he meant. "My parents used to bring me here on picnics, when I was little. I thought it was a wonderful place to swim. It was only when I was older that I understood the significance of it."

"And what is that?"

She was sure that he knew as much about this place as she did. "It's a sacred refuge, the ancient home of an *ali'i*, a ruling chief. Defeated warriors could take refuge here and their enemies couldn't harm them. People who had broken the *kapu* came here. The Hawaiians believed that breaking the sacred *kapu* offended the gods and the gods would react by causing lava flows, tidal waves or earthquakes. So if someone broke the *kapu*, he would be pursued and killed, unless he could reach this place."

Ross knew about the ancient legend, but he found himself drawn to the way she explained it with almost childlike wonder. "And if he made it here?" he prompted.

"A ceremony of absolution was performed by the *kahuna pule*, the priest, and all was forgiven. This was a place of life, where someone could find a second chance." Once again there was that faint wistfulness in her voice, that hinted at more than she wanted to reveal.

"Second chances," Ross repeated thoughtfully. He stood near the water's edge, his back to the small lagoon, the breeze lifting his hair from his forehead. He almost looked like an *ali'i* himself, with his black hair, dark skin, and air of command. Christina could easily imagine him presiding over a kingdom like this, just as he presided over the kingdom that was Fortune International.

At that moment she understood perfectly why Katherine had chosen him over everyone else to run the company. He had the steely determination, confidence, and strength that was needed to run a multi-national company like Fortune International, and to fight Richard Fortune and anyone else who attempted to take it away from Katherine. She knew he would fight her with equal determination. Suddenly she was frightened of him, and it was all she could do not to tremble before his relentless, probing gaze.

He asked, "If you really are Christina Fortune, is that why you came back? For a second chance?"

She was caught off guard by the question. It was far more perceptive than Ross could possibly imagine, and for once her defenses weren't strong enough to hide the turbulent emotions beneath the carefully controlled surface.

"I . . ." She stopped, then looked away, focusing on the *ki'i*—a stone carving standing on a rock in the shallow end of the lagoon—, the Great Wall that had once separated the palace grounds from the commoners' huts, the temple itself, *anything* other than Ross.

He persisted, "Did you come to San Francisco looking for some kind of sanctuary?"

Her thoughts went back twenty years, to that terrifying night when two young girls had tried desperately to find a safe place, not only from the man who chased them but from the shared nightmare experience that had driven them to the dangerous streets of New York.

"I don't believe that sanctuary exists anywhere," she whispered. "Not even here at *Pu'uhonua.*"

"What about forgiveness?"

Still not meeting his look, she said in a small voice, "That seems to be the most elusive thing of all."

She forced herself to look at him. There was a poignant expression in his eyes that revealed a vulnerability she never would have suspected he possessed. She was surprised to see that his own defenses were a bit shaky at that moment.

"How do *you* feel about forgiveness?" she asked. She was

uncertain exactly why the question had occurred to her, but as soon as she asked it, she knew she'd touched a nerve.

Anger glinted in those deep blue eyes. "As a virtue, I think it's highly overrated. Revenge makes a lot more sense to me than forgiveness."

"Then we have something in common."

Before he could question her further, she said, "I've had enough of interrogations for a while. I'm going swimming."

Turning her back on him, she pulled off the shorts and tank top, letting them fall on the sand, and kicked off her sandals. She was aware that he watched her as she raced into the water, splashing in the shallows, then throwing herself into the deeper part. The water was placid in the sheltered cove, with no breaking waves to impede her progress. With quick, sure strokes, she headed away from the beach, away from Ross and his disturbing questions and his even more disturbing presence.

She was careful not to swim out too far. She knew the current beyond the cove could be treacherous, and could easily carry her out to sea if she went too far. Gradually, she felt her body relax as the tension of their confrontation left her. The water was warm and clear. Beneath her, she could see schools of brightly-colored tropical fish swimming amid multi-colored coral. Turning around to face the beach, she treaded water and looked at the magnificent setting. Despite what she'd told Ross about sanctuary not existing anywhere, she felt drawn to this place. If there were such a thing as sanctuary, it would be here, in this lovely, serene setting.

Perhaps someday, if she accomplished what she'd set out to do, she could return here and try to find the forgiveness that had eluded her for twenty years, that had kept her heartsick in a way that nothing could alleviate.

Perhaps.

She saw Ross sitting on the beach, watching her. Her arms and legs were tired now, and she decided to return to the beach. But as she swam toward Ross, who stood there, waiting for her, she wasn't at all certain if she was swimming toward sanctuary—or danger.

✿   ✿   ✿   ✿   ✿

SEASON OF SHADOWS

by Mary Mackey

author of A GRAND PASSION and THE KINDNESS OF STRANGERS

A spellbinding and intimately wrought story of love and friendship, passion and purpose, revenge and redemption, and of the choices that irrevocably alter a woman's life.

Lucy and Cassandra were polar opposites: light and dark, pretty and plain, cautious and wildly impulsive. But from the first day they met at a Colorado prep school, Lucy and Cassie became the best of friends. Roommates at Radcliffe during the turbulent sixties, they stood by each other as Cassie seduced the man of her dreams and Lucy succumbed to David, the fiery poet who broke her heart. When beautiful blond Lucy meets Mila, the dashing crown prince of Patan, she must decide if she can learn to love a man who promises her everything, even though she has never forgotten David.

It was April, and outside Adams House the chestnut trees were in bloom. Inside, Lucy and Mila sat naked on Mila's new bed, their arms wrapped around one another, listening to sitar music. The music flowed up and down invisible hills, tracing a distant geography that seemed both remote and wonderful. Mila's body, too, was a path into mysterious places. Lucy rested against his shoulder, feeling warm and safe and more or less at peace with the universe. Mila was an amazing man: he knew more about loving than she had ever imagined a man could know, and yet, at the same time he was her companion and her friend and she grew closer to him every day.

The music stopped, leaving resonances in the air; the candle sputtered and flickered; when the silence was perfect again,

Mila rose to his feet, crossed the room, and opened the closet door. Bending forward, he became part of the shadows; the muscles in his back rippled like the muscles of a dancer. He straightened up, turned, and walked back toward Lucy holding a small white box. The box was ivory, inlaid with gold. On the sides and lid, Patanese court ladies from another century sat beside a pool filled with swans and lotus blossoms.

"For you," he said, placing the box in her hands.

She examined it in wonder. Every detail was perfect, right down to the tiny feet of the ladies and the sharp beaks of the swans. She'd never seen anything so finely made. She turned the box over and discovered the small red seal of the artist stamped on the bottom: two fish swimming under a quarter moon. "Thank you," she said softly, awed by its perfection. "I don't know what to say. It's absolutely beautiful."

Mila sat down beside her and ran his finger over the lid of the box. "I'm glad you like it." He smiled. "It belonged to my mother."

"Are you sure you want to part with it?"

"Open it," he suggested.

She lifted the lid and there, lying on a pillow of blue satin, was a diamond necklace. Matched perfectly, the strands of diamonds sparkled like a chain of fire. "My God," she gasped, "you can't be serious. I couldn't possibly accept a present like this."

Mila picked up the necklace, held it for a moment in the palm of his hand, and then fastened it around her neck. The diamonds were cold on her bare skin, and she shivered as they touched the base of her throat.

"Marry me," he said. He put one finger over her lips. "No, don't tell me you can't because I'm a prince and you're a commoner. That sort of prejudice is ridiculous; it belongs to another world, one that died centuries ago. I am not going to let my family select a wife for me. I have learned here in

America that love is completely democratic; love doesn't care about money or social class or what other people will say. I'm speaking from my heart, and I'd say the same thing if I was the poorest peasant: I love you, Lucy. Marry me, and I'll do my best to make you happy."

She stared at the fire in his eyes and the pleading in his face, and she thought a hundred thoughts, none of them coherent. For the first time in her life she had the sense of being on the edge of some kind of destiny greater than herself, and it frightened her. She loved him, she didn't doubt that any longer, but when she tried to imagine herself leaving her own country to live in Patan, she felt a chill of alienation. She couldn't see herself as a princess. The idea of wearing a crown seemed almost laughable, like something out of a child's storybook. And there was something else, something she hated to admit even to herself: she still loved David. She didn't want to, but she did; David was buried in her flesh like a fish hook, snarled around her soul, and she kept trying to struggle free and never quite succeeding. It wouldn't be fair to Mila if she married him and only give him part of herself. She felt a long pang of regret; she loved Mila in so many ways, but not enough . . . "I'm sorry," she stuttered. She reached up to take off the necklace, but the clasp seemed stuck and her fingers didn't work right. "I can't marry you. It's not possible."

"Why not?" Mila's face changed suddenly as if a cloud had passed across it.

"Because," she paused, looking for words to soften the blow, "because even though I love you, I don't love you . . . enough to marry you."

"Is that the only reason?"

"Yes," she whispered. "I'm so terribly sorry."

To her surprise he looked relieved. "But you like me, yes?"

"Of course I like you, Mila. You and Cassie are my best friends in the world." She felt terrible. Her eyes burned with tears.

He took her hand in his and held it for a moment and there was a long silence. "In my country," he said at last, "we believe that liking is what is important. Love for us isn't the same as it is for you. Here, in America, you sing for it as an uncontrollable passion that sweeps the lovers out of their ordinary lives and transforms them, but love for us is more like the music of the sitar: it doesn't rush toward a climax but grows slowly and almost invisibly like a great tree. For us love most often comes after marriage." He smiled ironically. "It's strange I should be saying all this to you because, you see, I love you in the Western way. Yet I am asking you to love me in the Eastern way—to marry me and trust that your heart will follow."

"And if it doesn't?"

"It will, I promise you."

She looked down at the box in her hands, at the ladies sitting beside the pool listening to distant music, and she knew that she had to tell him the ugly, plain, unadorned truth. "I was completely in love once, with someone else—a poet."

Mila's face tightened and he let go of her hand. "Oh," he said, "I didn't know. What was he like, this poet?"

"Unkind, crazy, not very dependable."

"You suffered?"

"Yes, I suffered."

He seized her hand again. "I hate this man who made you suffer; the thought of anyone causing you pain is unbearable to me. I would like to take him and strip him and tie him to a thorn tree and let the wild tigers feast on his intestines."

The thought of David stark naked waiting for the tigers had an undeniable appeal. Lucy smiled despite herself. "Thanks, but that's probably not going to be necessary. The last I heard he was out in San Francisco destroying himself with drugs, and no tiger could do a better job."

"Good," Mila said grimly. "I'm glad to hear that, because you're going to be my wife. I will defend you against all suffering, and any man who causes you the smallest pain in the future will regret it a thousand times over."

She started to protest again, but he wouldn't let her. "I don't care what your past is or how many wicked poets you once loved. I only want you now, in the present, and I warn you, I'm a very determined person who has been terribly spoiled. I'm used to getting what I want, and I want you, Lucy, my dear friend. I'll win that heart of yours."

"I wish that were true." She suddenly felt sad and lost and a bit ridiculous, and she wished—not for the first time—that she had never met David Blake. Taking off the diamonds, she put them back in the box, closed the lid, and sat for a moment looking at the ladies and the swans. How innocent they seemed; how she longed for that kind of peace. "I'm not sure I have a heart left."

"You wonderful woman!" Mila cried, embracing her. "Of course you have a heart! You don't believe me? Then I'll prove it to you." He kissed her hands and her neck and her bare chest. "Here it is, right here. I can feel it beating. I know that heart of yours; I know your goodness and your noble nature. And if you are really convinced that you can't love anyone completely ever again, then I know how to cure that. I know where the love in you is hiding, and I know how to make you feel it."

"Mila, don't; it's just no use."

"You think I'm making wild promises that I can't keep. But you're wrong. I can keep them."

Lucy gave up. It was useless trying to reason with him. She wished he could do everything he promised, but he obviously had no idea what he was up against.

FANFARE

FANFARE

Rosanne Bittner

_____ 28599-8 EMBERS OF THE HEART . $4.50/5.50 in Canada
_____ 29033-9 IN THE SHADOW OF THE MOUNTAINS
                      $5.50/6.99 in Canada
_____ 28319-7 MONTANA WOMAN .... $4.50/5.50 in Canada
_____ 29014-2 SONG OF THE WOLF .... $4.99/5.99 in Canada

Deborah Smith

_____ 28759-1 THE BELOVED WOMAN .. $4.50/ 5.50 in Canada
_____ 29092-4 FOLLOW THE SUN .... $4.99/ 5.99 in Canada
_____ 29107-6 MIRACLE .... $4.50/ 5.50 in Canada

Tami Hoag

_____ 29053-3 MAGIC .... $3.99/4.99 in Canada

Dianne Edouard and Sandra Ware

_____ 28929-2 MORTAL SINS .... $4.99/5.99 in Canada

Kay Hooper

_____ 29256-0 THE MATCHMAKER, ... $4.50/5.50 in Canada
_____ 28953-5 STAR-CROSSED LOVERS .. $4.50/5.50 in Canada

Virginia Lynn

_____ 29257-9 CUTTER'S WOMAN, ... $4.50/4.50 in Canada
_____ 28622-6 RIVER'S DREAM, ... $3.95/4.95 in Canada

Patricia Potter

_____ 29071-1 LAWLESS .... $4.99/ 5.99 in Canada
_____ 29069-X RAINBOW .... $4.99/ 5.99 in Canada

Ask for these titles at your bookstore or use this page to order.

Please send me the books I have checked above. I am enclosing $ _____ (please add $2.50 to cover postage and handling). Send check or money order, no cash or C. O. D.'s please.

Mr./ Ms. _____

Address _____

City/ State/ Zip _____

Send order to: Bantam Books, Dept. FN, 414 East Golf Road, Des Plaines, IL 60016
Please allow four to six weeks for delivery.
Prices and availablity subject to change without notice.   FN 17 - 4/92

FANFARE

Sandra Brown

- ☐ 28951-9 TEXAS! LUCKY .... $4.50/$5.50 in Canada
- ☐ 28990-X TEXAS! CHASE .... $4.99/$5.99 in Canada
- ☐ 29500-4 TEXAS! SAGE .... $4.99/$5.99 in Canada
- ☐ 29085-1 22 INDIGO PLACE .... $4.50/$5.50 in Canada

Amanda Quick

- ☐ 28594-7 SURRENDER .... $4.50/$5.50 in Canada
- ☐ 28932-2 SCANDAL .... $4.95/$5.95 in Canada
- ☐ 28354-5 SEDUCTION .... $4.99/$5.99 in Canada
- ☐ 29325-7 RENDEZVOUS .... $4.99/$5.99 in Canada

Deborah Smith

- ☐ 28759-1 THE BELOVED WOMAN .... $4.50/$5.50 in Canada
- ☐ 29092-4 FOLLOW THE SUN .... $4.99/$5.99 in Canada
- ☐ 29107-6 MIRACLE .... $4.50/$5.50 in Canada

Iris Johansen

- ☐ 28855-5 THE WIND DANCER .... $4.95/$5.95 in Canada
- ☐ 29032-0 STORM WINDS .... $4.99/$5.99 in Canada
- ☐ 29244-7 REAP THE WIND .... $4.99/$5.99 in Canada